The Five Daughters of the Moon

The Five Daughters of the Moon

Five Daughters
of the Moon

LEENA LIKITALO

A TOM DOHERTY ASSOCIATES BOOK

NEW YORK

THE FIVE DAUGHTERS OF THE MOON

Copyright © 2017 by Leena Likitalo

Cover art by Anna and Elena Balbusso
Cover design by Christine Foltzer

Edited by Claire Eddy

A Tor.com Book
Published by Tom Doherty Associates
175 Fifth Avenue
New York, NY 10010

www.tor.com

Tor® is a registered trademark of
Macmillan Publishing Group, LLC.

ISBN 978-0-7653-9542-9 (ebook)
ISBN 978-0-7653-9543-6 (trade paperback)

First Edition: July 2017

For my husband, Matti

Acknowledgments

I have always loved reading acknowledgments. They tell the story of a dream coming true, that of a writer becoming an author.

Hence, I will start my acknowledgments from the very beginning. I want to thank my family, my mother and father and sister and brother, for reading to me when I was too young to understand letters, but old enough to get lost in the countless stories shared with me during the long Finnish winters.

I want to thank my friends for listening to the stories I made up in my turn and all my teachers for trying to make me pay attention to grammar and correct spelling. Even though I only learned the importance of accuracy (and may have become slightly obsessed with it since then) once I fell in love with mathematics.

At this point, I want to thank Patrick Rothfuss for writing *The Name of the Wind*, the novel that inspired me to start taking my writing seriously. And then, right after this, I really need to thank my husband for not laughing at me when I told him that I wanted to quit my then day job and become a writer. We gave it a go. It didn't work out, but I'd like to think we learned a lot not only about writing but also about life in general.

I received my due pile of rejections, hundreds of emails bearing grim news. I was close to giving up on multiple occasions. But there were people who believed in me, who told me to keep on trying. Ann and Jeff VanderMeer, thank you for being there for me, for encouraging the novice writer who had big plans to go for it, even though she didn't yet know how to write properly in English.

Thanks are also due to my Clarion instructors and fellow classmates. During the six intense weeks, you taught me how to see the flaws in my writing and how to address them. For that, I'm eternally in your debt!

I want to thank Writers of the Future, the organizers and volunteers, my fellow contestants (especially Randy Henderson and Megan E. O'Keefe), and of course the judges. Very special thanks go to Kevin J. Anderson who connected me with my wonderful editor, Claire Eddy, whom I shall thank in this very same sentence for being the best editor ever. Thank you!

At this point, I was working on a different novel. When *The Five Daughters of the Moon* first came to me, I thought it was going to be a short story. The feedback from my dear Clarionites helped me to see that this story was never going to be happy confined in five thousand words. I think I wrote the first full draft in around two months to hit the Codex Novel Contest's deadline—these thanks are for the Codex writers who helped me to iron out the manuscript! I also want to thank Inka for all the lunch breaks spent talking about twentieth-century building materials and whatnot and being my consultant in everything Rafa and Mufu related.

Big thanks of massive magnitude go to my agent, Cameron McClure, who tells me what I need to hear instead of what I want to hear, and as a result ensures that my stories reach their full potential. I would also like to thank the hardworking people at Donald Maass Literary Agency, especially Donald Maass and Katie Boutillier, all of you, who have been my companions on this wonderful journey.

I want to express my gratitude also to the amazing team at Tor.com that has taken such great care of my duology: Carl Engle-Laird, Kristin Temple, Katharine Duckett, and Mordicai Knode. I love the covers the super-talented Balbusso sisters drew and the design by Christine Foltzer! The covers are beyond stunning!

I'm immensely grateful that I haven't had to travel this long and winding road alone. There are many more people than I can possibly list without risking tendonitis who have helped and inspired me. Hence, if you've ever read or listened to one of my stories, if you've ever given me advice or gently prodded me in the right direction, if you've been there for me when I've struggled to find the right words or chose the wrong ones, if you've seen me from close or from afar, but thought of me—this last thank-you is for you.

Thank you!

Chapter 1

Alina

"The Great Thinking Machine can answer every question," Gagargi Prataslav says as he steps forth from the shadows cast by the huge machine. Everyone in the audience, me included, shrinks back in the wicker chairs, for the gagargi is an intimidating sight in his black robes, with the hood half concealing his heavily bearded face. His dark eyes glow with the secrets from the world beyond this one, and not even Mama, the Crescent Empress, can endure his gaze for long. "It can find an answer to questions that no one has even thought to ask yet."

There is something wrong, so very wrong, in the way he speaks, the way Mama, my sisters, the guards, and the assembled nobles all listen to him. I don't want him to utter a single word more, but I'm two months shy of my sixth birthday. I don't yet have a name, no right for an opinion, even though my father is the Moon.

"Being built to do so"—Gagargi Prataslav motions at the machine looming behind him. The horrendous mechanical creature is as tall as three men standing on each other's shoulders, as wide as an imperial locomotive. With hundreds of pistons akin to sinewy, spindly legs pressed against its sides, it looks like a giant spider poised to strike. I don't want to see what sort of web the machine might weave—"it can be said that the Great Thinking Machine can, if not tell, then at least estimate the future very accurately indeed."

Light fades. The pavilion's unwashed glass walls and ceiling reveal that thick, gray clouds have gathered in the summer sky. Nurse Nookes would chide me for thinking it an omen, but she's back at the Summer Palace. Though two dozen guards in the blue and silver of the Moon protect me and my family, I suddenly feel very lonely and vulnerable.

I shift on my chair to nudge Merile, my favorite sister. She's only five years older than me and remembers what it felt like to not have a name. But now she perches on her seat, brown fingers curled around the linen of her frilly dress. She nods at every word the gagargi says, and the black ringlets piled atop of her head bob with the movement. Only the beautiful dog on her lap, Rafa, turns to look at me. Her other companion, silver-gray Mufu, sleeps curled against her feet.

"Future," Gagargi Prataslav says, stretching the pause between words as if he could control time, too, "can be pieced together from the clues of today."

I reach out to pet Rafa's head. She's a small, lean dog with chocolate brown eyes and big floppy ears. She meets my gaze with a deep, serious look. In this crowd, she's the only one who seems to understand my distress. Though gagargis have served the imperial family for a millennium, the way Gagargi Prataslav speaks implies that he wants something more. I have no idea what that might be.

At last Gagargi Prataslav bows. The hood of his black robes cascades to cover his face, and only the tip of his hawkish nose peeks out. Then he straightens his back with a flourish of his hand. His robes shift as though he were facing a storm, and the hood falls to rest against his back. His oiled black hair is braided tight against his skull. "Please let me present to you Engineer Alanov, the father of the Great Thinking Machine."

As the audience's focus shifts from the gagargi to a mere engineer, the awful spell lifts. Merile hugs Rafa, glaring at me for daring to pet her dog without permission. My older, even sillier sisters, Sibilia and Elise, resume gossiping. They look almost identical in their white dresses and plumes decorating their red-gold hair, but then again, they're of the same seed. Celestia, the oldest of us, leans to whisper in Mama's ear. Out of the Five Daughters of the Moon, she resembles Mama the most, and only she can glimpse the world beyond this one. Even now, the faraway look in her blue eyes reveals she's seeing more. One day, she'll be the Crescent Empress, the woman married to the Moon, and then she'll see what he sees, too.

"Your Highness, I'm greatly honored by this opportunity." Engineer Alanov's voice bears a tremble of a man told "no" one too many times. He is gaunt, and his thinning brown hair seems to be running away from his pinkish forehead. He keeps gazing at the mossy floor tiles, and his round glasses hang too low on his narrow nose. Inevitably, he fails to capture the audience's attention.

As polite chatter and court gossip fill the pavilion, I can't help wondering if I just imagined what happened before. For surely Mama would never let Gagargi Prataslav address her if she thought there was even the slightest chance of foul play. No, she wouldn't. Mama is wise and just. Under her rule, the Crescent Empire has only grown in size and prospered beyond anyone's wildest dreams—we have won many glorious victories against the kings and queens and other persons with titles I can't be bothered to remember because none of them are of heavenly descent like us.

Then I *feel* Gagargi Prataslav's stare, searing hot like a bonfire ready to devour witches. My every muscle stiffens, stomach knots tight, and throat shrinks. I manage to keep my attention riveted to the engineer only barely. Nurse Nookes claims that whatever I find so frightening, it really doesn't exist if I don't acknowledge it. I bet she's never met the gagargi up close.

"I have designed this machine to search for patterns in information and solve computational problems." Engineer Alanov's voice comes from far away, as if he were not really present. As if no one else but the gagargi and I existed.

Pretending to fan my face, I glance at Gagargi Prataslav from over the edge of my palm. There is something disturbingly hungry in the way he studies me. I'm neither foolish nor bold enough to meet his gaze, to find out if it's just my imagination playing tricks on me. Nurse Nookes claims that that happens often enough.

"And what need would I have for this machine?" Mama's question comes as a relief to me. Her gaze is bright blue, though this pavilion and everything it contains has fallen into disrepair. I don't know why she agreed to the gagargi's invitation in the first place or why I and my sisters were required to be present. Then again, there are many events where we must be seen but not heard.

Engineer Alanov glances at Gagargi Prataslav as if seeking encouragement or permission. The gagargi pats him on the shoulder, bony fingers coming to rest on the engineer's simple gray coat. Engineer Alanov nudges his glasses up and continues with a newfound vigor. "Information ... the machine can comb through and combine information from multiple sources. It can remember up to one thousand numbers at once, and it can perform the four main arithmetic operations:

addition, subtraction, multiplication, and division. The machine accepts numerical data and instructions as inputs, and it is capable of performing a multiplication of two numbers with up to twenty digits in *less* than three minutes."

Engineer Alanov blushes with pride. Sibilia and Elise burst into giggles. They're already old enough—Sibilia fifteen and Elise sixteen—that neither of them will ever have to worry about calculating anything. However, based on what they've told me about numbers, three minutes sounds like a short time to spend on pondering the possible results. They sure spent much longer agonizing over the tasks assigned to them.

Mama raises her right hand minutely at Elise and Sibilia, and my sisters manage to stifle their giggles. Mama nods, and for a moment I'm not sure whether she did so because she's pleased with my sisters or because the engineer has caught her attention. At last she says, "I have plenty enough accountants already. They have the finest calculators and fastest fingers. What need would I have for this machine of yours?"

Engineer Alanov sways as though Mama had just slapped him. The flush on his cheeks deepens to scarlet as he glances again at the gagargi. Gagargi Prataslav smiles. His teeth are white, but slightly crooked. They remind me of . . . Well, if a wolf's fangs were filed even . . . But no, this is the sort of description that Nurse Nookes would chastise me for, or worse, force me to swallow another spoonful of her foul potions.

"For efficiency. People tire and make mistakes." Gagargi Prataslav produces from inside his robes, from a hidden pocket, a pack of cards—ordinary playing cards? He picks one up and holds it so that the weak light can flow through the neat arrangement of holes. No images or words or numbers tarnish the surface. "These cards contain instructions for the machine, and the machine never disobeys."

"It is full of holes," Mama says in a tone that indicates that not even a blind person could have missed that. Or not even Elise and Sibilia, no matter what they're gossiping about.

"Holes, yes!" Engineer Alanov claps, his fingers all knuckles and chipped nails. "The arrangement of these holes forms the language that the Great Thinking Machine can read ... and write. Every one of these cards is a program, and every one of these programs has been written to solve a specific problem. But, note that one program can be run against unlimited sets of data. For example, I have here a program that simulates intelligent redistribution of resources ..."

Mama flicks her forefinger to silence the engineer. Her crescent platinum ring gleams, but the shine is somehow dull. As is Mama's voice. "Let us discuss more relevant cases. I assume you can write new programs to solve new problems."

Gagargi Prataslav's gaze darkens once more, and when he speaks his voice is veiled by a sweetness that reminds me of the honey Nurse Nookes uses to cover the bitter aftertaste of her potions. I hate honey. "The Great Thinking Machine can accomplish more than a mere human mind can ever even imagine."

I can see people around me, Mama included, stiffening once more. It's as if they were slowly turning into stone. The pavilion's moss-laced glass panes dampen what remains of the light, and what little reaches us is not enough. Yet no one else seems to notice this.

I pinch myself. Twice, and hard enough to leave bruises. I must be imagining again. I know I am, and if I speak of this ... I will only embarrass myself.

"I have looked into the past and present. But neither of

them hold the solution for the problem we face." Gagargi Prataslav strolls to brush the machine's side as if it were a steed about to set foot on a racing track. He pats it two times in quick succession. The metallic echo is hollow. "In this changing world, with its more complex problems, to find the right solutions, one must look into the future or perish like the beasts of the olden times."

I don't like this future the gagargi describes. How dare he, how dare he speak as if Mama really needed him and the machine to rule her empire! She should tell him to say no more. But she doesn't. She listens to him intently.

I can't take it anymore. I push myself up from my chair and jump down, as nimbly and silently as only a girl of my age can. Rafa abandons Merile's lap to accompany me. Only then does my sister stir.

"Where . . . where are you going?" Merile asks, drowsily as though she'd just woken up from a nap.

I nod toward the door at the far end of the pavilion. Let Merile think I'm feeling weak again. And maybe I am. That must be it.

"For the sake of the argument, let me pose a simple question," the gagargi says, turning to face Mama and Mama alone. "Who fights the hardest: a soldier with his stomach full of rye bread or one starving because promised supplies never arrived? Who works the hardest: an unfed or nourished peasant?"

Rafa and Mufu trot past me, to the door, nails scratching the cracked tiles. They halt there and glance over their shoulders. Their eyes, so big and soulful, glint with concern and caring for their mistress and maybe for me, too. They want us to leave this place.

"Trivial questions, are they not?" From the corner of my eye, I catch the gagargi studying me. He must have heard the dogs moving. "The key to the door that stands between us and the luminous future is the intelligent redistribution of resources."

"Fine." Merile gets up slowly. She brushes her white hem straight, runs a hand over her hair to ensure the pins still hold her ringlets in place. They don't, but she merely shrugs. "I'll come with you."

"Engineer Alanov, if you will?" Gagargi Prataslav pats the engineer on the shoulder, much like he patted the machine. His pleasant smile bears a hint of cruel amusement, and I know, just know, that that smile is targeted to me. It says: *Run, run if you want to, but you can never flee from me.*

The engineer clears his throat, maybe fearing that the rest of his audience might trickle out after Merile and me. Sibilia notices us leaving then. She whispers something to Elise, who then whispers the message onward to Celestia. My oldest sister turns her head so minutely that the ibis-bead tiara resting against her tall forehead doesn't shift at all. Her gaze radiates the kindness she feels toward her every subject-to-be, including me.

Merile takes hold of my hand, and together we dash out. A pair of guards joins us at the doors. A Daughter of the Moon is never truly alone. Though, with my sisters to look after me, that's not something I need to ever fear.

Merile hums under her breath as we walk along the gravel path circling the pavilion. Nobody else lives on the Gagargi Island apart from Gagargi Prataslav and his flock of apprentices. From this side of the island, with the pavilion blocking the view, I can't see the Crescent Island or even one of the many towers of the Summer Palace. The view to the ocean is unblocked. The sea breeze carries a hint of things rotting. Farther out in the sea, sheets of rain fall down from coal-black clouds. Seagulls screech as they swoop the skies, but they keep away from the shores of this island. Only a fearless magpie, the bird black and white, dares to prance on the rocks.

We turn a corner. Rafa and Mufu dash through the tall grass, all arched backs and slim limbs. But suddenly they halt, one forepaw in the air. Then I catch a glimpse of the peacock corrals and swan pens in the valley below.

"Go on, silly dogs," Merile says to Rafa and Mufu. To me she says, "The wings of the pedigree birds have been clipped."

As Rafa and Mufu run down the hill, toward the corrals and pens, I think of the poor birds. Of course I know where the soul beads come from and that the gagargis must practice their art somewhere. And yet . . . I shiver as I glance over my shoulder. Though the gagargi's brick house with its massive round towers looms at the far end of the island, the shadow stretches longer than it should, almost far enough to touch me, though that's impossible. And I'm not imagining it. "I don't like this place."

Merile tilts her head sideways, and the black ringlets bounce with the movement. Out of my four sisters, she's the only one who takes my worries seriously. But as she's grown, as I've grown, even she has changed. Maybe soon she, too, will report my words to Nurse Nookes or, even worse, directly to Mama.

"Why . . ." But before Merile can say whatever she was about to say, what I didn't want to hear anyway, the barking of dogs, shrieking of birds, and flapping of broken wings distracts her. And me, too.

Merile grins, not old enough to be above mischief after all. She glances at the corrals, to catch a glimpse of dog tails and raised heads, clipped wingtips and curved necks. "I should call them back."

But she doesn't.

We stroll along the long side of the pavilion. Only the dirty glass separates us from the audience gathered in a semicircle to listen to the gagargi speak. We pass the guards, the audience, even the gagargi. The glass muffles his voice, for which I'm happy. His words are poison.

The machine looks as massive as ever. Merile runs her fingers against the pavilion's wall, parting the thick, green moss to reveal the glass underneath. She rubs her thumb and forefinger together. Her white glove is ruined. "Elise's governess, she told her that this used to be a greenhouse. She says every gagargi has his own area of interest. Specialty of one sort or another."

As we turn another corner, I think of the machine, less threatening now that the glass stands between us. Is the machine Gagargi Prataslav's specialty? Or does he do something else, too, here on this island that no one in her right mind would want to visit?

"What is he doing now?" Merile wonders aloud. She tiptoes closer to the pavilion's wall. I follow her through a bush of lupines, and so we both hover as close as we dare, squinting through the panes.

Engineer Alanov stands but meters away from us, his back against the wall. Before him is a sturdy table, on it a polished wooden box. He inserts a key into the heavy iron lock. As he props open the box, an amber glow lights up his weasel face.

"What is that?" I ask, even as the engineer lifts from the box a bead the size of my fist. He turns around swiftly and marches to the machine.

"It can't. It can't be . . ." Merile whispers. "Mama would never allow that!"

The engineer opens a hatch in the machine and lowers the bead in solemnly and carefully. He steps back, head bent down and arms crossed behind his back like a country gagargi retreating from the altar. A heartbeat later, the machine screeches, a high-pitched sound from an unoiled throat. The insect legs burst into a gallop. The pistons and wheels and cogs—I think that's what they're called—join the movement.

I shriek back, stumbling on the lupine stems. I cling to Merile's arm before I notice what I'm doing. Out of the corner of my eye, I notice our guards staring at us.

"The machine . . ." Merile's mouth hangs slack. She looks around for her dogs, then at me. It's almost as if she's seeking someone to comfort her. But that can't be. She's eleven already! "The machine has come to life."

I've seen things come to life before. But these things have been small and insignificant, toys created for our entertainment or novelty items meant to buy Mama's favor. Nothing this big. Or threatening. Merile and I really should go. But I don't dare to say a word for fear of alerting the guards. For that would lead to them reporting to Mama.

Behind the glass, Engineer Alanov inserts holed cards into the machine. He licks his fingers at regular intervals, presses each sheet down with great care. The machine looks hungry even after he finishes. I know for sure, no matter how many beads and sheets he'll feed the machine, it can never be fully satisfied.

"Come." Merile tugs my hand, and I'm overjoyed to obey her. My sister leads me down a path toward the shore. Rafa and Mufu appear from amidst thistles, run to us, bounce next to us, tongues lolling out from between tiny, sharp teeth. The guards tail us from a distance.

I can't speak for as long as I hear the awful machine shrieking. Merile and I walk down a hill, toward the ocean. It might rain soon. If it does, we need to return. But . . .

"I don't want to go back," I say as we halt on the rocks polished smooth by wave after wave. From this side of the island, I can see home, but this does little to comfort me. Strange as it is, it's the presence of the magpie, the same one I saw earlier, that gives me the courage to speak. "The machine . . . it looked so hungry."

Merile squats before me and places her palms on my shoulders. Dove beads glitter around her neck, against her brown skin. They remind me of the amber bead the engineer fed to the machine. Which animal's soul was that one?

"My dear sister, you have nothing to be afraid of."

But I have. The machine looked so terribly, terribly hungry. The gagargi's gaze was so dark. He has plans for me, I know that for sure.

Everyone knows that without a name a soul can't anchor to the body, and I still have to wait two more months for my name. The gagargi, I'm sure of it now, he wants to feed me to the machine. That's what his cruel smile meant.

"What is it?" Merile asks, brushing my cheek as I blink away tears.

The magpie studies me, head cocked to the side. The two guards pretend they don't see me crying, though no doubt they took note of that. I'm once more ashamed of myself, my fears that I know are more than that. But how can I voice them without sounding ridiculous? How do I tell my sister without alarming her? I don't want her to run and report to Nurse Nookes.

I whisper, "What if I lose my soul before my name day?"

Merile glances over my shoulder at the guards. They stand with their backs straight, rifles leaning against their shoulders. Dust doesn't stain their midnight blue uniforms, nor does it mar their black boots. My sister flicks her finger at them, and they take ten steps back, just enough to give us privacy but still be able to protect us from whomever might want to hurt us. Though even they can't protect me against the gagargi, not when his words turn people to stone.

"A secret," Merile says. "If you tell me what name you've chosen, I will keep it a secret."

What she is proposing is . . . My heart gallops like a three-legged wild pony. Nurse Nookes would definitely chastise me if she heard of this. And Mama wouldn't approve, for it's still two more months until the ceremony. I really should wait.

"I can't . . ." It would be so very wrong. And yet, and yet I have known for months already what I want to be called when I finally turn six.

"I told my name to Sibilia. And she told hers to Elise. Who told hers to Celestia," Merile reveals. She squats farther down and takes hold of my hands. Her fingers are so warm, even through the stained satin. "And nothing bad happened."

The sea breeze is getting colder, heavy with the rain to come. I shiver as I stare up the hill, at the pavilion, and through the glass at the machine. I can hear it rumbling, puffing steam. I can't see Mama, my sisters, or anyone else in the audience. But the machine can see me. And it still looks hungry.

"Alina," I whisper in Merile's ear, and it feels to me as if I were somehow, impossibly, sealing my fate. "My name will be Alina."

Behind us, the machine screams a protest. But it can't have my soul. My soul is now anchored to my body.

Chapter 2

Merile

Smell. I could smell everyone present in the grand hall even with my eyes closed. The favored nobles with their perfumes and colognes, bergamot oils with a hint of lavender and amber undertones. The servants carrying refreshments, sparkling white wine and bite-size sweet pastries in more sorts than I care to count. The omnipresent stink of horse sweat and gunpowder that ever clings to the high-ranking soldiers. And then . . . then there's the sharp, thorny scent of the gagargi that always confuses both me and my dear companions.

"Tonight is an important night." Gagargi Prataslav reaches toward the sky beyond the grand hall's glass ceiling. Dressed in his ceremonial black robes, he looks taller and more powerful than I've seen him ever before. For a moment, I think he might really manage to touch the clouds that hide the Moon. Then he slowly folds his fingers into a fist, lowers his hand before him. Though I know what's to come, my skin goes to goose bumps. It's five years since I got my name, but it's a day that one can never forget. "The Moon shines benevolently upon us."

I stand on the raised stage with my sisters and dear companions, in a crescent arc behind Mama, Gagargi Prataslav, and our youngest sister. The nobles dressed in the shades of the Moon, officers of the imperial army, and servants alike stare at the trio, regardless of why they're present. Though I can see only my sister's back, the gray-brown hair held in place with dove pearls and the white, silver-sequined, long-sleeved dress that looks slightly too large even though three different seamstresses took it in on three separate occasions, I can tell she feels more out of place and nervous than I did on my name day. Whatever potion Nurse Nookes tricked her into swallowing isn't strong enough.

Mama, regal in her ermine-trimmed gown, smiles in approval as the gagargi uncurls his long, bony fingers. A white bead the size of my fist rests in the cup of his palm. For some reason, at that moment, I think he holds the whole world in his palm, though it's just the soul he needs for the naming spell. Rafa nudges me, her nose cold and wet through the silk of my dress. Though I'd normally pick my dear companion up and coo at her, I don't, for this is a solemn ceremony. But Rafa was right to rebuke me for the ridiculous, childish thought. Mama is the Crescent Empress. Everything under the Moon belongs to her. And after her, that same everything will be Celestia's, for she's the oldest Daughter of the Moon.

I fix my attention to my little sister just in time to see the gagargi bend toward her, closer than is necessary. Blackness. Not even one glimmer of silver breaks the blackness of his robes, and so he is akin to a storm cloud or a rogue wave. My heart goes out to my little sister.

"Honored Daughter of the Moon," Gagargi Prataslav says, leaning even closer. The hall is only dimly lit—the chandeliers bear egret beads—and in the swan bead's white glow, what little skin remains visible from under the gagargi's oiled beard bears the paleness of one who rarely steps outdoors. His thin, colorless lips remain parted as if he were reluctant to continue.

Or as if he were displeased by something.

As the silence stretches on, people in the audience shuffle toward the stage regardless of their rank or lack of it. For this is an important moment not only for my little sister but also for the whole Crescent Empire. Though my little sister is the youngest, she's fifth in the line of succession. Poor Mama never had sisters.

Another nudge against my calf. This time it's Mufu. She's getting impatient, too—her thin black tail wags like a pendulum of a clock gone mad. Still the gagargi won't continue. I want to order him to do so, but it's not my place to say a word. Mama's pose remains regal. She looks calm from behind, but I can't help wondering if a flicker of annoyance mars her expression.

At last, Gagargi Prataslav says, "What name have you chosen for yourself?"

My little sister—she's told me her name, but I don't dare to address her with it yet—glances shyly at Mama. We're not fully human before our sixth birthday, not before we get our name. Officially get our name. No one is, and this is how it has always been, even for the Daughters of the Moon.

Mama nods sagely. With her pale hair pinned up, with an ibis-bead crown circling her head, she looks ethereal, dreamy, as if she existed not only here, but also in the world beyond this one. She turns to face my little sister, and the scent of her perfume tickles my nostrils. White roses in bloom. Curious that she still wears her summer perfume.

"My name is . . ." My little sister shivers. I've heard the servants whisper that she chose a bad month to be born. Her name day falls in the second month of autumn—on any other year we would have left for the Winter City already. Maybe the crowd's anxiety is partially caused by that.

"Yes, my child?" Mama prompts, gently brushing my sister's shoulder. As an empress, she would never display impatience of any sort in public, but she must want the ceremony to be over and us on our way to a warmer climate. This city was designed to remain cool during the summer months. It's autumn already, and come winter, everything here will freeze.

My little sister crosses her hands over her heart. She whispers shyly, "My name is Alina."

From the corner of my eye, I catch Celestia nodding, Elise and Sibilia hastening to follow her example. I do likewise. My dear companions, Rafa and Mufu, nod too. The light brown head goes down as the black head goes up. They're so silly.

"Alina." Mama is the first to repeat the name my little sister has chosen. It rolls off her tongue smoothly. No one has a voice as full and pleasant as hers, one that stirs your heart and summons you to obey, no matter what the request may be. "Let her name anchor her soul to her body."

"Alina." Gagargi Prataslav repeats the name, but from his lips, it sounds jagged. I don't understand why. Nurse Nookes says that only the gagargis and empresses are without fault, devoted as they are to serving the Crescent Empire. "Veneered Moon, hear the name your daughter has chosen."

The crowd of favored ones, those who have been chosen to witness the sacred ceremony, stills in anticipation. Even my sisters and I stare fixedly at the gagargi as he lifts the soul bead up once more. He pronounces the sacred spell under his breath and lets the bead drop. As the bead connects with the black stone tiles, the glass cracks. For a moment, there's nothing but shards.

Sea after rain. I can smell the swan soul before I see it, the moist scent of the sea after rain. Then a white shape, no bigger than the bead was, forms before Alina, at her feet. Thickening wisps spin into a shape: powerful wings, arched neck, black beak. The swan spreads its wings wide, flaps briskly. Rafa and Mufu shuffle back. They hide in the cover of my voluminous hem. I remember more vividly than is proper how it felt to stand there, feel myself become whole, a person.

"Honored swan, the sacred messenger of the Moon." Gagargi Prataslav sails to stand behind Alina, black robes billowing. As the swan regains control of its wings, the gagargi spreads his arms wide and his sleeves brush the floor. His voice, strong as a gale wind, touches every nook and corner of the grand hall. I must be imagining it, but it almost sounds as if it hides a hint of displeasure. But how could it?

He says, "Bear the name Alina through the clouds and the sky, to the night that blesses us after day. Let the Moon know the name of his daughter. Let the Moon be proud of his child."

Alina sways as if she were about to faint. I hear one of my sisters gasping in concern—Elise or Sibilia, I think, but I don't dare to glance at them. Rafa and Mufu whimper from the depths of my hem as the swan takes to the air. It soars over me and my sisters, circles up, toward the domed ceiling. For a moment, I'm sure the glass panes will hold it back, or that they will soon shatter.

But the swan's soul passes through the panes as easily as if nothing had ever held it back. I stare after the bird, the receding white dot. Clouds part before it, close in after. All too soon, it becomes just one more speck of light, a faraway star, and I think . . . Are all the stars swans, messengers of the gagargis? Do they sing to Papa of good and bad, of what has come to pass in the empire he's bestowed upon his wife to rule?

"My dear daughter," Mama congratulates Alina. She pecks a

kiss on both her cheeks, but lightly, so that her reddened lips don't leave marks. I can't recall the last time she displayed such warmth toward any of us. We see her but an hour a day, for running the empire keeps her occupied from dawn to dusk.

At last, I dare to steal a glance at my sisters. Celestia, as pale and fair as Mama, beams in ethereal approval. Elise and Sibilia, each fair of skin but merely pale compared to her, whisper to each other. I'm darker of blood, and so is Alina, but only mildly compared to me. There are rumors in the court—I've heard them, for people are often careless around those who don't have a name or have acquired theirs only recently—that Mama's choices for our seeds are political, that it suited her to pick mine and Alina's from the Southern Colonies.

"This gift," Mama says as she accepts a gold-engraved box from an attendant draped in midnight blue. She holds it up for everyone to see, and light slowly returns to the hall as servants unveil owl-soul lanterns. "It is from General Rasvatan. He sends his fondest regards from the Southern Front."

Alina stares at Mama, her big brown eyes round with confusion. It's as if she's not really here, but seeing things that exist only in her mind. How can Nurse Nookes's potion be wearing off already?

"Poor thing," Sibilia whispers to Elise as she fidgets with her long sleeves. She insisted they be made of lace so thin as to appear almost translucent, but that may not have been the best call. The fabric seems to itch. "Not to have her seed present at her name ceremony."

"Hush." Celestia nudges Elise, who proceeds to nudge Sibilia.

I feel bad for Alina only. Rafa must sense it, for she rubs her head against my knee. Since the most important part of the ceremony is over, and since I'm only eleven and hence allowed some leeway, I pick my companion up and clutch her against my chest. Mama should have summoned General Rasvatan to the court. She could have done so. Why didn't she?

Alina's small hands shake as she holds the box, though it's only the size of a thick book. Whatever the box holds, it's bound to be immeasurably valuable. Though it can't contain anything living. I press a kiss on Rafa's forehead and inhale the lovely scent of her fur. My seed gave me the best name day gift possible—my dear companions!

"I can't wait to see what she gets," Elise whispers to Sibilia, though we're not supposed to prattle during the ceremony.

Hesitantly. Unaware of our curiosity, Alina lifts the lid slowly, almost hesitantly. She holds the box so that only she and those standing right behind her can see what it contains. Elise strains her neck. Celestia elbows her once more. I hold my posture. There's a limit to what I can get away with before Nurse Nookes is forced to reprimand me.

"Oh!" Alina lowers the box as an intense blue glow escapes from inside it. Her mousy gray hair lights up in shades of indigo. Her pallid skin turns even more so. "It's . . ."

Mama steps to her side. Slowly and regally, she picks up the object from inside the box. General Rasvatan's gift is a blue-and-green-enameled miniature peacock. Its feathers are crafted to lifelike perfection, but where its belly and chest should be gleams brightness in a cage of gold-netted glass.

"Is that a . . ." I whisper under my breath, hoping one of my sisters can impede my curiosity. Rafa shivers against my chest, but Mufu, rather uncharacteristically the braver of the two, lifts her forepaw. She'll go and investigate if I give her the permission to do so. I don't.

"It's a soul-automaton," Sibilia replies without moving her lips. She must fear Celestia's elbows, though there's no way our sister could reach her without making a scene. And that's something someone as serene as Celestia would never do in public.

The attendant in midnight blue retrieves the box from Alina. She sighs in what can only be relief. Next to her, Mama turns the tiny golden screw under the peacock's tail. Alina stands very still as the automaton comes to life, and I can't help thinking that it's as if my sister doesn't realize that the spell is already fueled by the peacock soul, that she thinks that she must cease to be for the bird to be!

The mechanical peacock sings a chiming, vibrating tune. Alina trembles. She'll soon burst into tears. Elise must have reached the same conclusion, for she rushes to embrace our sister from behind. Mama's brows lift, but she nods at Elise as if her presence were indeed required by the ceremony.

"A gift fit for a Daughter of the Moon," Gagargi Prataslav announces, clearly pleased by the general's choice. He has his arms clasped before him, but hidden by the voluminous sleeves.

Alina barely glances at the peacock. Her tight smile is one I recognize too well. She's very afraid of something. But of what, I can't say, and I can't ask. For the time has come for the rest of the court to present their gifts to Alina.

———

"Have you seen Poet Granizol?"

Sibilia pauses munching the éclair only when she wheels around to face me. Beautiful blush covers her round cheeks.

Powdered sugar dusts her plump lips. She swallows and pats her mouth in a napkin embroidered with the crescent motif. "Ummm . . . sorry? But, have you seen the servant with macarons lately?"

Sibilia and her obsession with pastries . . . Sometimes she's just as bad as Rafa and Mufu, who continuously beg for treats. I rise to my toes to crane past her into the dance hall, and my dear companions echo the movement.

Inside, Elise swirls from the arms of one handsome young man to those of another. Dressed in a white gown with a high, silver-sequined waistline and a hem so light it follows her every movement, she looks akin to a young swan. Her red-gold hair curls into a crown of its own, the weaves held together by plumes and dove pins. Her laughter chimes even above the court gossip and the waltz the string quartet plays.

"Sixteen," I whisper under my breath. Our sister is beautiful, carefree, and admired by everyone. "If that is what it's like to be sixteen . . ."

"It is!" Sibilia sighs, palms pressed against her heart. Of course she'd be the one to know. She's but one year away from the magical age. "This year simply can't pass fast enough."

We watch, mesmerized, as Elise dances. When the song comes to an end, she curtsies to her current partner, then turns around to choose her next one from amongst a half dozen or so admirers.

"If I were her, I'd pick Count Albusov." Sibilia nods as if agreeing with herself. "Sure, he might be bald and a bit on the skeletal side, but look at the plenitude of soul beads sewn into his coat. I've heard his estate is one of the largest in the whole empire!"

For a moment, it does seem like Elise will favor Count Albusov, though he must be twice her age. But then, a dashing young captain with his copper brown hair tied into an elaborate topknot boldly strides past the count to our sister. He's muscular in the lean sort of way, and his midnight blue and silver uniform fits him so perfectly that he must be blessed by Papa himself.

"The nerve of him . . ." Sibilia gasps. Both Rafa and Mufu turn to look at her. I don't, for then I'd miss the action on the dance floor.

Everyone. Everyone has paused to stare at the scene around our sister. The orchestra, bows hovering above the strings of violins and cellos. The couples with hands wound around each other. The older ladies and lords standing on the sides of the hall, holding drinks raised to their lips or about to spill them. And then there are the very people involved in what is about to turn into a major faux pas. Count Albusov's bald head positively glows with his shock at this disregard for rank. The young captain completely ignores this, and . . . he bows at Elise swiftly, but elegantly.

Our sister glances at Count Albusov, then at the young captain. She lifts two fingers to her lips and smiles so radiantly that no matter how she'll choose, no one can think ill of her. She lowers her hand, brushes her hem in a way that leaves it girlishly swaying. And then, she favors the young captain with the tiniest of nods.

"She can't!" Sibilia stomps the floor twice, and Rafa and Mufu bounce back to the shelter of my hem. "She simply mustn't approve of that sort of behavior."

Too late. Elise has made up her mind. As the young captain offers her his hand, she accepts it. She places her hand on his shoulder, white kid glove against the silver epaulet. He draws her closer, his hand on the small of her back. As if it were in his right to lead a Daughter of the Moon, to demand anything, let alone . . . intimacy. A violin sings the first note of the waltz, and it's too late, too late to do anything.

"Oh no . . ." For quite some time Sibilia is lost in her thoughts, no doubt imagining the chastisements Elise's disregard for court etiquette will rain upon us. Then she shrugs, and her red-gold eyebrows lift as if she'd just remembered that I still wait for her answer. Her skirts swoosh as she squats down. As she pats my shoulders, her white gloves ooze the scent of honey and chocolate. "Come to think of it, dear Merile, I haven't seen Poet Granizol since the ceremony."

I sigh, and Rafa and Mufu sigh with me. But my companions get over their disappointment much faster than I do. Mufu rises to her hind legs, more interested in what might remain of the éclair than my distress. Sibilia shakes her head at my companion. As she pats her head, a red-gold curl escapes from behind her ear. She notices the stain on her glove, shrugs, and lets the curl remain as it is. "And you're out of luck, too."

A servant with a tray laden with tiny butter-crust pastries—apples and almonds, by the smell—ambles past us, so overwhelmed by the crowd that he doesn't notice Sibilia and me. Both Rafa and Mufu, however, turn whip-fast, to stare after him in hopes the man might fall and a blessed avalanche of treats tumble upon them.

"Luck," I remark, aiming my words at my apparently completely gullible and bribable companions. "We're all out of luck."

"Oh, Merile, don't be sad." Sibilia, still squatted down, leans toward me, ready to hug me if need be. Her white gown clings to her skin, to her round bosom, to tell the truth. Though she's already fifteen, she wears a dress more akin to mine than to Elise's or Celestia's. Ours have high necklines and long, tight-fitted lace sleeves. I like my dress, but on Sibilia... She's a woman dressed like a girl.

"I'm not sad," I say.

"He must be somewhere here..." Sibilia trails off as she spots a servant to our right with a tray full of macarons. The silver reflects the red and green and yellow promises of sweetness. My sister swiftly gets up. She casts one last glance at the dancing Elise, then an equally longing one at the macarons. "Do you want me to help you look for him?"

Sibilia doesn't ask why I want to find my seed, and I don't want to tell her. She's not particularly fond of hers. General Kravakiv has been off fighting for the empire since she was born anyway.

"No," I reply, and, released by my word, she sails away toward the sugary salvation of macarons.

Grand hall. I can't find Poet Granizol in the grand hall and neither does he loiter in the hallway leading into the older, colder parts of the palace. But it's in this hallway that I detect the faintest hint of bitter smoke, and though I shouldn't wander off alone, I do. Either the guards will shadow me or then they won't. I'm not worried—no harm can fall on me on the palace grounds, no matter what Nurse Nookes might think.

The crowd thins as I leave behind the rooms where the guests plot and gossip and dance as is the way things have always been here. I pretend not to see people holding hands with the wrong people, stealing kisses, swaying away, locking doors behind them. Rafa and Mufu trot beside me, nails clicking against the plainer floor tiles. They sneeze at the sticky smell of the many perfumes mixed with sweat. I follow the scent of smoke, for I know I will thus find the Poet.

Right turn. Down a narrow corridor. Left turn. The farther away I veer from the grand hall, the more the temperature drops. Coldness seeps through the soles of my slippers. My breathing turns into white clouds.

"Children are not tarnished by personal pursuits or the other faults that come with a name."

Anywhere. The voice is faint, and yet I'd recognize it anywhere. I stumble to a halt. Rafa and Mufu bump into my legs, tangling into my hem. What is Gagargi Prataslav doing here, so far away from the center of the party?

I've never liked the gagargi—something I share with Alina—and I'm not particularly keen on seeing him now. But I do want to know with whom he's talking, for I suspect he might be up to something.

Gagargi Prataslav's Great Thinking Machine devours human souls, though no one wants to believe it. That is, Elise laughed at me when I told her what I'd seen, and cautioned me that if I were to make such a joke before anyone else I'd soon find myself sipping Nurse Nookes's potions. After that, I didn't have the courage to mention what I'd seen to anyone else, and the next day I learned that Mama had rebuked the gagargi's plan, thank the Moon!

But now, Gagargi Prataslav might have other plans. I sneak farther down the corridor lit by duck-soul lamps.

"I knew upon first seeing you that I could place my trust in you. You are wise beyond your years. Many times wiser than those who have made so many unfortunate decisions in the past." A pause. Someone must have replied to the gagargi. "Indeed, what those who criticize progress don't see, what you saw straightaway, is that the Great Thinking Machine is a gift sent by the Moon himself."

Closed door. The gagargi's voice comes from the room at the corridor's end, from behind a closed blue-paneled door. My fingers tingle with excitement and ... I glance over my shoulder, wishing that a guard had indeed trailed after me. There's no one around but Rafa and Mufu. Yet my curiosity is stronger than my current uneasiness. I tiptoe to the door, my companions right behind me, nails scratching the tiles until they halt with me. After a moment of hesitation, I peek through the brass keyhole. Surely if the gagargi can't see me, he won't know I'm listening.

"We teeter on the edge of two ages." There's no mistaking Gagargi Prataslav, with his thick, oiled braid resting against his back. However, I'm more curious as to whom he's talking to than what he's preaching about. Unfortunately, the gagargi's figure blocks the view, and I only catch a glimpse of a white gown. That's not helpful at all, for most ladies honor Papa tonight by wearing the shades of the Moon. "The time has come to decide whether we want to be a part of the new age or fade away with the old one."

I tilt and turn my head to better see, my eye so close to the brass that its cold surface stings my cheek. To no avail. Rafa nudges me, sensing my frustration.

"The Great Thinking Machine has crunched through the numbers. The Crescent Empire has reached the optimal borders. There is no need to expand upon what is enough to provide for all those who have worked so hard for the good of the empire. Let there be no more pointless campaigns, young men yanked from their bright futures, good women and children starving to provide for useless military excursions."

Strange. These are strange things that he speaks of. But what do I know of what goes on behind closed doors? Politics are for Mama and Celestia. All that is expected of Elise, Sibilia, me, and Alina is to . . . well, we are the Daughters of the Moon. We can do mostly whatever we want, barring endangering the succession, whatever that might mean in practice.

"It is not lightly that I have bestowed these words on you." Gagargi Prataslav strolls toward the lady in white. His movements are smooth, but grim, akin to those of an alley cat approaching a mouse. And he ends up standing too close to her, looming over her. "You will consider my words."

A statement. Not a question. I strain my ears to hear the lady's reply. With each pounding heartbeat, I want to know more dearly who she is. But before she can reply, the gagargi flinches. He angles his head as if he were the one listening now. Then he spins around, to face the door.

I stumble back, and my companions retreat with me. The gagargi, the holy messenger of Papa himself, possesses knowledge from the world beyond this one, from the realm of shadows. He has many powers, maybe some that I don't know about. He might have sensed me spying on him!

"There you are." A hand that reeks of smoke grasps my shoulder from behind. I stifle a shriek. But Rafa and Mufu yelp in joy. Their tails wag wild. "My darling little Merile."

Relief washes over me as I recognize my seed, the Poet Granizol. He's a big man with what Elise calls a perpetual tan and eyes as black as onyx. She would also call his scarlet, gold-embroidered coat garish. She wouldn't deign to comment on his green, reptile-leather boots.

"Here." I clutch his arm. Rafa and Mufu trot away from the door. They sense my need to flee the scene. And flee I must before the gagargi comes to investigate these sounds. "I was only here looking for you."

Poet Granizol sways as I lead him down the corridor, toward a corner and away from the line of sight the gagargi would have from the door. Mufu sneezes. I hold my breath.

"And now you've found me, my shine of a star," the Poet announces, impervious to my wish to move faster. Loud. He's so loud! "You shouldn't have looked for me from so afar!"

I can hear sounds from the door behind us, a key moving in the lock, the handle turning. I hasten my steps, trying to reach the corner before the door opens. Though a horrible thought occurs to me: if I can hear these sounds, then the gagargi might have heard me talking to the Poet too!

"I . . ." I try to come up with a lie. But my throat is parched. "I'm thirsty."

"But of course." The Poet's gait steadies as though his life had a purpose now. "A flower needs water to grow, rain and sunshine to bloom. Come, my little Merile, I know just the room."

When we finally turn around the corner, I risk a glance behind us. The door is just about to open. We made it.

Of course we made it. I'm a Daughter of the Moon. Papa looks after me from the sky.

"I see the seed I sowed in the fertile soil of the empire has taken root well and grown into true beauty. There, I couldn't have said it better." The Poet leans back on the plush blue sofa of the smoking room. The corners of his onyx eyes wrinkle, and his wide smile reveals his impeccably white teeth. Handsome. I've heard ladies whisper that he's handsome to look at. I've heard with my own ears that he's a fine speaker. But I've also been told by my sisters on numerous occasions that the only sharp object he can wield without being a danger to both himself and others is a pen, and since even his skills with a pen are highly debatable, he would be so useless at the battlefronts that Mama never sends him there.

The Poet pats a silver-tasseled cushion, and if anything has ever bothered him, there's no sign of that tonight. "Do sit down here where the velvet whispers."

I grin, and Rafa and Mufu grin too, pink tongues peeking out. They rub against my calves, and I no longer worry about the gagargi. Even I had a hard time tracking the turns my seed took as he led us into this room. I take a seat next to him. My companions curl against my feet.

"Is it the shine of the Moon himself that I see in her innocent eyes?" The Poet waves his hand in a wide arc, golden rings gleaming around every single finger. He stares theatrically at the ceiling, though I doubt he admires the paintings there, as the sickly sweet smoke veils the whole room. Just as we can't see the other people in the room, the smoke also hides us, and my seed and I are just two shapes occupying one of the many sofas. "I know it without a doubt, she will grow very wise."

I giggle at him. Sibilia says the Poet has got his tongue stuck in honey and coated with sugar. She claims the Poet flatters everyone, but I don't care what she says. She might just be envious. Her seed is always at the battlefronts, never here.

"My gift!" Poet Granizol claps. His rings clink as they meet. Rafa and Mufu stir to this sound. Mufu's floppy ears perk. Then she sneezes again. "Have you found them to your liking? Or are you disturbed by their occasional licking? Ah, they truly look fine tonight! You must have brushed them with all your might."

I beam. I did brush my companions myself, and personally chose the collars. The chain of oval diamonds complements the shine of Rafa's silky hazel fur. The dove pearls shine lovely against Mufu's dark gray coat. To me, they look more elegant than Elise, who spent the whole evening before her mirrors. Though that I would never say aloud, lest she'd tell Nurse Nookes, and I'd be the one disciplined.

"Fine are the creatures I chose for my seed. Now, where is this one thing I dearly need?"

I watch the Poet pat through his pockets, amused. He has a way with words. Will I have that gift too when I grow up? That would be wonderful. I could put an end to my sisters' teasing for good.

"Ah, there it was all along. For a moment I thought it truly was gone." The Poet produces a silver cigarette box from his pocket, a gift from Mama when he was still in her favor, I've heard. He flicks the lid open and fumbles to pick up a cigarette. He's already about to light it when he glances at me, grinning as if he were a scullery boy about to do something forbidden. "You don't mind if I smoke, do you?"

The smoke in the salon is already so thick that I can't see past my own extended hand. Besides, I don't understand why he's asking my permission, of all things. It's not as if I really matter. And yet, I nod.

"She was always full of nos." A tremor runs through the Poet's body. His fingers tremble as he produces a flame from the silver lighter. This trembling eases only after he's sucked the first taste of the acrid smoke. "Though that is not a word she knows."

He's talking of Mama, I guess. But since I don't know for sure, it's better not to reply. I pat my knee lightly. Mufu replies to my summons instantly and jumps on my lap. My darling companion.

"Ahh . . ." The Poet smacks his lips, eyes closed. His lashes are long and black. I hope mine will grow to be like his, for in comparison, even Elise's are short and pale. "Never does this taste better than on a night blessed by the Moon himself."

I watch my seed smoke in silence. Rumors. There are almost as many rumors about him as there are of me and my sisters. He was Mama's favorite once, but only for a short while. These days he's rarely invited to the court. Though many share his vices, I've been told Mama can't tolerate his. I bury my fingers between Mufu's collar and her fur, seeking comfort from the warmth. I don't want to anger my seed, but there's so much I don't know. So much I want to know.

"What is it that you are smoking?" I ask, for to that he can answer honestly at least.

Poet Granizol turns his back to me before he puffs more gray clouds. When he's done, he leans toward me, elbows against knees, onyx eyes wide. "The nectar for those who need to imagine, for those who yearn to see more. For those who are afraid, but bold enough, to glimpse the world beyond the great door."

The Poet's words make no sense. Rafa and Mufu glance at him, too, sharing my opinion. Maybe seeking out my seed wasn't such a good idea after all. Maybe I should return to the grand hall. Sensing that I'm about to get up, Mufu jumps on the floor.

"Don't go." The Poet lowers his hand on my arm. His fingers feel hot through the fabric of my sleeve.

"Mama might need me," I say, although that's not the truth. The court celebrates Alina tonight—though, given how shaky she was earlier, she has no doubt retired already. As in all the celebrations, everyone has their eyes set on Celestia and Elise. Sibilia and I don't matter. That's the role of the younger daughters. To be ignored and forgotten. But Mama can't possibly understand any of that, as she's the oldest and only daughter.

"The empress is akin to a celestial object or a distant star. She can only be glimpsed from afar. Oh, when the planets align right, terrible, terrible is her might."

As I shake my head, the world blurs around the edges. Rafa nudges my shin. Mufu sneezes. I feel cold. "I'm not sure I feel well."

The Poet touches my forehead, the wrinkles on his brown forehead deepening. "I will read you poems. A nourished soul can never fall ill."

I debate with myself whether to leave or stay. If I leave, I might faint. If I stay . . . I don't see my seed that often, and he did give me Rafa and Mufu. I decide to stay.

"Here, lay your head on my lap. This one is called 'The Ode to the Moon, the Light of the World Beyond This One.'"

I close my eyes and let myself lull into the trickle of his carefully chosen words. As I inhale more smoke—there's no avoiding it in this room—the words swell into a stream, then into a river. I float in my seed's gentle voice. The words, they have no meaning, never had. All that matters is that I'm with him and that he cares the most for me, and not one of my sisters.

Suddenly the Poet falls quiet. A heartbeat later Rafa growls and Mufu joins the warning. I jerk up to a sitting position, just in time to see the smoke part and a ghastly figure emerge.

Gagargi Prataslav strides toward us. The heels of his boots

clack loudly against the floor. His black robes billow behind him as if he were riding the wind. His dark eyes gleam with pure malice.

Frozen. I sit on the sofa, frozen, head spinning. My companions hide in my hem. The gagargi knows I eavesdropped on him. He might know more than that. How? I can't say. It doesn't matter.

"A Daughter of the Moon," Gagargi Prataslav says as he halts before the sofa. His thin lips form a smile. Why he's smiling, I can't tell, but I scoot instinctively toward the Poet. The gagargi shakes his head. He says to the Poet, "Go."

The Poet glances at me, at the gagargi. I cast a pleading look at my seed. *Don't go!*

The gagargi's smile deepens until it becomes a scythe's edge. I know now where I've seen that expression before. On a cat toying with a mouse. What can he be thinking?

The Poet opens his mouth as if to argue. He's noticed how I clutch my hem. He may have heard how my heart thunders.

"Go," Gagargi Prataslav repeats, and his gaze darkens. He has much power. He's to be feared.

The Poet gets up. He doesn't look at me. Disappointment and anger pierce my heart, leaving me wounded beyond recovery. I can't believe how easily he gave up on me. "Fine." He sucks in another breath from his cigarette. He exhales it toward the gagargi. "But I'll be back."

Gagargi Prataslav laughs, a deep rumble from his chest. I hunch on the sofa. Rafa peeks out from the cover of my hem. She hesitates but a moment before she jumps to take the Poet's place. My brave little companion. I hug her against my chest. I don't even know why I feel so threatened. The palace is full of people; just there, on the other side of the room, older ladies gossip and decorated soldiers exchange war stories. I suspect.

"Now, little Daughter of the Moon." The gagargi arranges his robes. He smooths the folds one at a time before he takes a seat too close to Rafa. My dear companion whips her head around to growl at him, needle-like teeth bared.

"Why . . ." Gagargi Prataslav pats Rafa on the head, though she pulls her ears back, tight against her slender neck. But as soon as the gagargi buries his bony fingers into her smooth hazel fur, she stills. The growl dies in her throat. "There is no need for ill will. None. None at all."

Mufu, still hiding in my hem, trembles. She buries her head against the underside of my knee. But even that doesn't make me feel better or braver.

"Look here, yes here, little Daughter of the Moon." Gagargi Prataslav speaks softly, in a melodic tone that could pass for a grisly lullaby. I don't want to listen to him, but how could I not? I obey.

The gagargi holds in his hand, the one that he's not petting Rafa with, an empty glass globe the size of Alina's fist. I know immediately what it's used for. I saw one but hours earlier. A tremor that has nothing to do with the room's temperature runs down my back.

"Yes. It is an empty soul bead," the gagargi says, his voice deceitfully friendly. With his middle finger, he draws a circle on Rafa's forehead. My throat tightens, and I barely dare to breathe. Mufu nudges me, nose cold through the layers of my dress. "How should I fill this emptiness? What do you think, little Daughter of the Moon?"

I shake my head so vigorously that the pins holding my hair up loosen and the beautiful creation unravels. He wants to, means to, take my friend's soul to fuel his foul spells. I know that without asking.

"You can't . . ." I manage to whisper. But my voice is weak. As insignificant as I am.

He laughs again, as if pleased by my terror, and his gaze deepens. He cradles the empty soul bead in his palm, precariously from side to side. "I cannot what?"

The words get stuck in my throat. He can't have my companion's soul. That's what I want to say. But as his stare bores through me, vicious, I shrivel. I shrink in the sofa. Rafa is limp, as if in deep sleep that precedes death. There's no escape. The gagargi can take whatever he wants, and I can do nothing to stop him.

The gagargi inhales, grin baring his crooked teeth. I realize he enjoys my distress. He's a cruel man. How he ever managed to climb into Mama's favor, I can't fathom.

"Merile . . ." Celestia's voice comes from far away, pure and chiming and spun from silver. Then I see her—and I don't know how I didn't notice her sooner—gliding toward me. "What are you doing here, of all the places?"

My oldest sister takes in the scene, the predatorial lunge of the gagargi, my shrunken posture. She's tall and serene, white as winter in her gown, with the diamonds and pearls forming an ethereal glow around her. She clicks her tongue, but her expression remains otherwise indecipherable.

"Honored Celestia." Gagargi Prataslav rises up, gloating as though her sudden arrival pleases him immensely. As he lifts his fingers from Rafa's forehead, my companion stirs. Rafa glances around, confused, as if she doesn't know where she is or how she ended up on the sofa. I sigh a cooing sound of relief.

"Go," Celestia says to me. There's an undertone of urgency in her voice, as if she isn't quite sure how long even she can hold the gagargi's interest. "Go now, my dear sister."

I flee. Rafa and Mufu run at my sides, treading on my hem. Their nails tear the silk. I don't care. I won't be wearing this dress ever again.

Spins. My head spins, and I shiver as I make my way toward the grand hall, up a stairway I don't remember taking earlier, down another. I need to talk with Elise or Sibilia. They need to know what happened, even if they might accuse me of lying. Maybe I should talk with Nurse Nookes, maybe even with Mama. Though they might not believe me. They never believe Alina either.

As I stumble down another set of stairs, into a thickening crowd, I hear snippets of conversations. I can't pinpoint who says what. Or understand. I can't understand what they mean either. Like waves. There are too many people around me, parting before me, closing in after.

"The Crescent Empress is akin to a shark: as that great fish must swim to live, so must she expand her empire."

"A shark, you say? Then what are the gagargis?"

My vision blurs, and I can smell only the smoke the Poet favors. I sway onward, toward the open double doors that lead to the grand hall. Elise. I will find Elise there. Surely this time she'll believe me!

"The gagargis have always been a part of the empire. I say she should not have rejected the Great Thinking Machine without at least trying it. What does it matter if it consumes souls? We have plenty of war prisoners waiting for good use. Plenty of orphanages and workhouses filled to the brim."

I flee the words that don't make sense. Or maybe they do. I

don't know. The whole world is but smoke, and I forget . . . I'm fleeing the gagargi. I must remember that.

"We have been looking for you everywhere!" Someone grabs my hand when I'm but steps away from the grand hall's doors.

I shriek. Rafa and Mufu shriek too. It's the gagargi. He's caught up with me!

"Merile?" But no, it's just Elise and the young captain. Dove beads shine amidst her red-gold locks. The gagargi gave them to her as a gift. The gagargi . . .

"Gagargi," I stutter. But speaking of him only reminds me of the immense terror. Hurt. He wanted to hurt me. My dear companions. "Oh, Elise . . . The gagargi . . ."

Elise bends down and sniffs at me. Her pale gray eyes widen. She shakes her head, brows arching. "Have you been smoking something? Tell me, have you?"

What is she talking about? There are more important things to say. But I know the look on her face, the frown, the pursed lips. She won't listen to me now. I need to find Sibilia.

I yank myself free and spin around. Rafa and Mufu yelp as I stumble on them, in my hem. My left ankle twists. Something snaps, and pain lashes through my leg.

I fall on the hard parquet. People stop mid-sentence, to stare at me. Shame. I feel shame, but also terror and pain.

"Help," I whimper. "Elise, help me."

Chapter 3

Sibilia

Tonight, my dear Notes, I'm happy! Happy, happy, happy!

At last, you might be tempted to remark. Admittedly, I've been doing lots of complaining during this autumn, but who can really blame me? My sisters and I have been stranded in this cold palace for months now, with no end in sight to our imprisonment, since the unrests (whatever those are about) that have spread across the realm don't show any sign of calming. Here, the balls and concerts and fetes continue as before. Without me, since I have to wait eight agonizingly long months more for my debut.

No complaining today. Yes, I promised that, and if a Daughter of the Moon can't be held accountable for her words, then who can? Onward with the splendid news.

Today, I learned that I won't have to wait till I'm a shriveled old hag to take a lover, but that I may take one as soon as I debut. Praise Papa! Praise Celestia! And perhaps, since Nurse Nookes constantly reminds us that we live in troubled times, I might get away with getting a lover (one particular K, as you might have guessed) even before that. Though that would be scandalous. So very scandalous that I'm itching to do exactly that.

Loving a man before one's debut... Perhaps that's too

much to ask for. But a few more waltzes, some kisses and caresses, and . . .

Spilled ink. Now it's smudged all over the page. Sorry about
that, dear Notes. I will show more self-restraint in the future. I
certainly will.

How was my day? How did I come upon this great news?

Nurse Nookes was the usual pain in the backside. She in-
sists we stick to the same day routines, riots or no riots. So,
scriptures it was for me, hour after hour of reading and repeating the sacred texts and writing my reflections with the fountain pen that refused to run out of ink and release me from the
agony. Papa, forgive me, but I find the words you shared with
us before you rose to the skies terribly incomprehensible and
boring.

I must have drawn the short straw when Mama decided to as-
sign Nurse Nookes to look after me. Elise's governess, Lily, tells
her the latest court gossip. But Nurse Nookes—her cruelty
knows no limit! She makes me read the scriptures every single
day. Soon I'll know them by heart whether I want to or not.

A ghastly thought. Perhaps that's been her intention all
along!

Tonight I had enough. I lied to that wrinkled witch that my
stomach hurts (it does, since it's *that* time of the month. I can't
believe I ever looked forward to getting my *wretched* days). She
ordered me to bed. I pleaded her to fetch me a cup of hot
chocolate. She frowned at me, and for a moment I feared my
ruse had been revealed. Then she left. As soon as the heavy
thudding of her waddle faded, I fled.

The one good thing about the Summer Palace is that here
I only need to walk down one drafty corridor to reach any of
my sisters. My heart pounded wild (not as wild as it did when

I danced in secret with K at Alina's name day celebrations) as I tiptoed to Elise's door. I was sure Nurse Nookes would return at any moment. Luckily, she didn't, and I managed to sneak into Elise's room uncaught.

"Just in time! But do close the door before my precious heat escapes," Elise called at me from before her vast vanity table. Her red-gold hair, gathered in a chignon atop her head, glowed like a halo. She was dressed in a beautiful, silver-encrusted ball gown, but she hadn't donned her gloves. She didn't need them yet—the tile stove in the corner glowed with pleasant heat. "Could you fetch my dove pearls? The ones with the tangling diamond crescents?"

I pushed the door closed, but tilted my head in a way that stated I'm no servant, as my sister should know. There was a silver tray with an arrangement of different chocolates on the side table to my right. Though there were no beautiful bitter dark ones, I popped one in my mouth anyway. My luck had it that it had that awful berry paste inside it. Why, oh why are the cooks so stingy with chocolate these days?

"Pretty please?" Elise gazed at me, begging like Merile's rats might. Her dress did look terribly stiff with the heavy embroidery. She probably couldn't get up on her own.

I swallowed the rest of the chocolate and sighed. "I will, but just this once."

"Perfect!" Elise clapped her hands together and cast me her best smile, the one she's used to charm every single count and lord and captain she's ever met. Dear Notes, though she and I are of the same seed, I fear I will never manage to look as elegant as Elise. "I knew I could count on you! Believe it or not, I have a concert to attend, and I'm nowhere near ready to be admired by half the empire."

"Ah, the concert . . ." I had completely forgotten that Elise was going to an event tonight. Well yes, Notes, that's actually a lie. I knew very well that she and Celestia had accepted the invitation from Marques Frususka and were due to leave in an hour or so. K had been invited too—Lily had told this to Elise upon some prompting from me. "A friend of mine will be there, too."

"Great!" Elise clapped her hands again, but this time she studied herself in the mirror as she did so. She shook her head minutely. Then clapped again. She met my questioning gaze through the mirror. "What? Practice makes perfect. You should try it, too."

I could hardly contain my annoyance and envy as I brooded across Elise's room. Every single piece of her furniture—the bed at the alcove, the lush sofa with a round table before it, the massive wardrobe (though she naturally has a separate clothes room)—is made of mahogany. The carpets are white, as are the velvet bedcovers and the silver-embroidered sofas. Hers is a grown-up room. Mine still has a dollhouse in the corner, and though I've told the servants to take it away on multiple occasions, it always returns. Just as we don't really exist before our sixth name day, we're but children till we debut at our sixteenth.

"Sibs, what is it?"

Of course she was spying on me through her mirror. We, the Daughters of the Moon, are nothing if not cunning.

"Nothing." I yanked open the wardrobe's doors.

Countless dresses hung crammed in there, silk pressing against satin and chiffon. Each had carefully worked sequin, pearl, or soul-bead details. Every single one of them had a high waistline and short sleeves, some feather trimmings around the low necklines. One had a vine of hummingbird beads twining around the bodice. I would kill to get to wear that one in public. Swear to Papa I would.

Despite the wretchedly gorgeous dresses, Elise's jewelry box was impossible to miss—it's the size of my dollhouse, a lacquered construction with two dozen drawers, each etched and enameled with variations of crescent patterns. In his midnight blue uniform and ostrich-feather bicorner hat, K is impossible to miss, too. With that black hair of his tied in a bun and the grin-to-die-for on his tanned face, all the young ladies present in the concert will be swooning after him. Right at this very moment, I fear.

"You're a poor liar," Elise chided me, but still wouldn't get up from the stool. If I were the one invited to the concert, I'd be bouncing all over the room. But I'll have to wait till next summer, which is completely unfair. What if the recent restlessness spreads here, too? What if there will be no balls next year? What if K is simply no longer available then? What if someone else snatches him first?

"It's about that friend of yours, isn't it?"

Dear Notes, you know it too well, Elise always has to have everything. Nothing less suffices. At that moment, I was so truly worried about my sister stealing K that I pulled the drawers open like a burglar pressed for time. One after another.

"Oh, Sibs!" Elise called me as if I were indeed her servant. "In the bottom drawer."

It was then that I noticed it, with half of the drawers open already. Each was empty, or close to empty. No pearls lay on the velvet beds, no earrings waited to be donned, no bracelets to be slipped around slender wrists. My sisters and I, we have so many dresses that we often wear them only once before handing them over to our friends or servants. That's necessary, too, since they know the latest rumors and expect repayment in one form or another. But jewelry we never give away, especially soul beads, for the person such a piece is bestowed upon holds the responsibility for the souls and the power they contain.

I rattled the drawers as if I could thus by some miracle make the missing pieces reappear. I couldn't. There was but one possible explanation—someone had stolen my sister's jewelry!

"Where are all your jewels! We must call the guards at once," I blurted. And my heart jolted with excitement. A theft in the very palace. In my sister's chambers. Perhaps there could be some action in my chambers, too!

"What?" Elise froze, right hand poised to apply rouge on her freckled cheeks. She blinked slowly, working through what to say next. I know my sister well, but an emotion I couldn't quite name slipped through her composure. Worry or anxiety, perhaps? "No, we won't."

I glanced at the barren drawers, my slippered feet tapping the question I didn't dare to ask. Who was she protecting? Or was there something else at large?

"I sent them to be cleaned, silly Sibs." Elise met my gaze through the reflection, brows drawn sharper and raised as if that was obvious to begin with. "You'll find the dove pearls in the bottom drawer."

I curled my fingers around the silver knob, the metal cool against my skin. Something didn't quite add up. But to call a theft, that would cause trouble for everyone, and I like all of our servants.

And indeed, the dove pearls rested on the velvet of the bottom drawer, gleaming with the souls that the gagargis had coaxed from the birds. I picked the pearls up gingerly. If I were a thief, would I leave behind something this valuable? Nope. Not even if I was out of practice or a butterfingered novice.

A rustling sound interrupted my train of thought. Elise had got up at last. She clutched the hem that must have weighed a ton. She must have applied too much rouge, for her cheeks glowed brighter than fitted her. She kept her gaze down. "Will you help me fasten it?"

I dangled the pearls from between my fingers as I ambled to my sister. On the way, I bumped into the sofa. I lack the grace that comes to my sister so naturally. Or perhaps I haven't practiced enough before my mirrors. Notes, I'm writing it down here and hold you accountable for reminding me, I shall start practicing graceful gestures and movements at least once a day. No, make it twice a day.

Elise held her head down and red-gold hair up as I fastened the pearls around her neck. After I'd secured the clasp, she straightened her back. Of the flush I'd seen earlier, there was no sign. She took my hands in hers.

"Do you want to hear the latest rumor?"

"Depends," I replied, wary. She's my best friend, but she's also cunning. More cunning than I am in so many ways.

"The thing is, my dear Sibs"—she gave my hands a squeeze, but her voice wavered—"I think Celestia has a lover."

At first I failed to register the importance of Elise's statement. Then my legs gave in, and I would have ended up on the floor if she hadn't been holding my hands. "She . . . she has a lover at last?"

Elise hugged me tight. The sequins pressed against my chest almost painfully. How she could stand to wear the dress, even think to wear it all night, I couldn't even imagine. But I admired her for that.

"She's sneaking out all the time," Elise said as she detached from me. She ran a finger down the length of her necklace. "And there's this glow, a dreamy look about her."

I swayed, I'm afraid to admit this to you, as I pondered on this revelation. Could my eldest sister really be in love at last? If there had been a change in her, it had completely escaped me. Though Celestia has always been different from the rest of us, so regal and rational. Then again, she has to be—she will be the empress one day. We won't.

Unless she were to die, that is. Which isn't something I wish to happen, just to be clear, dear Notes, as that sort of statement will see one to an early grave or to an exile in the least.

"Perhaps Papa has finally taken note of our plight," I replied gingerly. During the past two months, I'd asked Papa to facilitate a romance with K often enough, not that I would ever admit that aloud either. "I thought he'd wait till we were all old hags."

Elise skimmed a step back and held her hands out for me. I clasped them.

"Come next year, come your debut," Elise said. We started spinning together as we sometimes did when we were much, much younger, both still wearing girl dresses. Now her dress, heavy with silver sequins, positively crepitated. My nightgown merely whooshed. "You can charm as many young men as you want. And for myself, I have just the right handsome young captain in mind."

I leaned back, smile widening with mad glee. For I could have K as my lover! At last! Unlike Celestia's, our lovers won't become generals and court officials by default. We are free to love whomever we choose, provided she picks a lover first and we maintain caution. For messing up the succession order never ends well. One only has to think of Mama's sisters and what became of them. They're . . . gone, as if erased from history.

I was so concentrated in thinking of this and basking in joy that I didn't notice Elise's intention to halt. And as she halted, I stumbled and collapsed with her.

"Elise . . ." I chided her, panting against her shoulder. The world still spun around me. "What was that?"

"I have an idea." Without offering further explanation, my sister pranced toward the doors leading to the balcony, despite the weight of her dress. When my sister spoke, her voice chimed with excitement. "Come!"

"Where?" I blurted, always, always so hatefully clumsy compared to her.

In Elise's room, pristine white curtains embroidered with crescents guard the balcony's double doors. Elise swooped her hands around them and pulled them apart. She turned the key twice in the lock and pushed the doors open. Night breathed in the chill of late autumn.

"Come now," Elise said, disappearing outside.

I followed her like a lamb. As the Daughters of the Moon, our lives are full of transitions. Name at six. Debut at sixteen. Death. Returning to the sky to shine next to our Celestial Father. What was following my older sister where she deemed fit compared to these?

The smell of algae and rotting leaves instantly flooded my nostrils, but I ignored it. The garden lay below, canals criss-crossing its length. At this hour, only the imperial guards haunted the tiled paths. And one untired magpie, it seemed.

The Moon peeked through the thin, gray clouds, and the guards' shadows mixed with those of the many willows and poplars.

"Dear Father Moon." Elise curtsied between giggles. I curtsied, too, heart beating with guilt and excitement. Nurse Nookes would chide me if she learnt of this. To sneak from my room, to fool around outside without a coat or gloves!

But Elise spread her arms wide, bent her head back, and addressed our father. "Please send us lovers, handsome and tall."

"Elise! You can't just . . ."

Elise glanced at me, grinning. She fluttered her painted lashes. "I can't just what? We are the Daughters of the Moon. We have the right to call out for his help when in desperate need."

At that moment, I did consider if I really was that desperate to meet K again. His lineage is impeccable; not that I care about that sort of thing. He adores me. I'm sure of that, though we shared only one waltz, in secret, during Alina's name day celebrations. But the look he cast me afterwards, from across the dance floor. Smoldering.

"Your turn." Elise elbowed me.

"Ouch." Dear Notes, my sister has the boniest, sharpest elbows.

Elise looked at me expectantly, and I knew it then: if I didn't ask something from our father, she would ask something much more daring in my place.

My voice was but a whisper, but this is what I said: "With curious mind and wandering hands."

Elise gasped, shocked by my plea, and I was pleased to see that. "Why, Sibilia . . ."

The guards in the garden below stirred to these sounds.

They glanced around, hands tensing around their rifles. In their sky blue uniforms and the black bicorner hats, they looked menacing, men ready to spring into action on our behalf. They hadn't yet spotted us, but inevitably . . .

I fled inside, Elise at my heels. She pulled the doors shut, while I blushed embarrassingly furiously. Perhaps I shouldn't have said what I did. Perhaps Nurse Nookes's diligence is my punishment for yearning for what I should wait one more year to have. But surely if Celestia has a lover, I can take one, too. What difference does a year make at this point anyway? I'm already a woman!

"Are you all right?" Elise asked. No matter how bossy she can be at times, she has a good heart.

I fanned my face—blush often creeps to my cheeks. Oh, that night with K, I was blushing all the time when we danced, but he seemed to find that charming, can you believe that, Notes?

"Sibs?" Elise placed a palm on my shoulder.

I really didn't want to let go of my fondest memories, but if Elise caught me dreaming, she'd extort the juiciest details in no time. "Um . . ."

A timid knock on the door saved me. Elise and I exchanged looks. Her right brow arched in question.

"It can't be Nurse Nookes," I whispered hoarsely, but yet I pondered if that old raisin really could sense when I was up to something.

Elise shook her head, and the white-gold crescents tangling in her chignon clinked. "It can't be. I sent Lily to keep her occupied. It must be Celestia."

But Celestia, the empress-to-be, would never knock. For a moment, I entertained the thought that Elise might have succumbed to the temptation and done the unthinkable—acquire a lover before our eldest sister had officially announced hers! She sure had shared more than one dance with that handsome young captain, what was his name again? Captain Janlav, I think.

The door slowly opened. But instead of our oldest sister, the visitor was the youngest. Alina slipped in, tears in her deep-set brown eyes, clutching both hands against her narrow chest. She wore but a nightgown and white slippers, as if she'd climbed out of bed midway through the night.

Elise and I glanced at each other. Not again. Dear Notes, sometimes it's hard to believe that Alina is our sister, a Daughter of the Moon. Not only does she look different from the rest of us—frail and vulnerable and borderline mousy—but this weakness seems to affect her mind as well. Most of the time it's harmless. She's just immersed in her own world, but when the concoctions Nurse Nookes brews wear off—or Alina has managed to spit them out in secret—then our youngest sister turns erratic.

Though dressed in a gown that must have weighed half of her own weight, Elise squatted down akin to a mistress waiting for her poodle to come and greet her. "What is it, dear?"

Alina dashed to Elise and fell on her knees before our sister. A sob shook her whole slender frame, from the gray-brown hair to the tiny lamb-fur-lined slippers. "Oh dear . . ." Elise glanced at me from the corner of her eye before she met Alina's tearful gaze. "Shouldn't you be in bed already?"

The balcony curtains remained parted, and the whole sorry scene was visible for the Moon. I didn't know whether I should go and draw them or not. Then again, a father deserves to know when something ails his daughters. And lately, a lot has been ailing the youngest.

"The sh... sleep won't come when it spies on us." Alina produced something shiny from the cradle of her hands and thrust it at Elise. When Elise cupped her palms to accept that something, I caught a glimpse of more details. Alina wanted to rid herself of a shiny blue-green object no bigger than her fist. "Take it."

"Alina!" Elise called out as she recognized the object. General Rasvatan had given the mechanical peacock to Alina. I tutted, too. How could Alina even think of passing onward the name day gift of her own seed?

"Can you take it?" Alina's gaze darted from Elise to me. I shivered, though the palace had rooms much colder than Elise's. How could my little sister look so gray and haunted? What was it that she was seeing? I wondered if we should call for Nurse Nookes, no matter the consequences.

Elise rustled up, shaking her head as Alina drifted from her to me. I stared at my little sister in something approaching horror. Alina was akin to a sleepwalker. But the dark circles under her eyes spoke a different story. She was wide awake, had been for hours. Or days. "Sibs, please, you take it."

I shouldn't have, but how could I refuse when distress so tortured her. I accepted the mechanical bird. It weighed more than I'd expected, and I almost dropped it. "But just for safekeeping."

Relief shook Alina as she rid herself of the peacock. She wrung her hands together and swayed from side to side. "Thank you! Thank you so much, Sibs."

As I turned the mechanical bird in my hands, I tried to understand what had so frightened my sister. The peacock was a marvelous gift that must have cost General Rasvatan more than he could have possibly afforded. Powered by a peacock soul, the mechanical bird could mimic the true bird in shape, form, and sound. I touched the spring under the bird's tail, about to wind it.

Alina twitched, shied away from me, toward the door. "Don't. Please don't."

Elise hurried to comfort her. The hem of her dress, so heavy, didn't follow her movements. That wasn't quite right. Everything always followed her way.

"Why?" I asked as this silly, creeping anxiety of theirs, the wrongness, started to bother me as well. Why, Notes, I can't tell. The bird was of a workmanship of the most magnificent kind. The enamel feathers so carefully carved. The claws decorated with platinum details. But it was the sapphire eyes I was drawn to. Like everything else powered by a soul, the peacock automaton had a life of its own.

"I can't sleep while it watches me," Alina replied, and then she was crying again.

Elise hugged Alina. She glanced over our sister's shoulder at me. I knew what she was thinking. Our poor, fragile sister, so sensitive, so frail. How could a seed from General Rasvatan result in such weakness?

Ashamed by my thought, I strode to the tile stove and hastily placed the bird on the sill, facing against the wall, as far away from us as possible. Then I hurried to join the embrace. Behind us, the Moon shone brighter, or that was how it felt. I prayed to Papa to make our sister stronger. A Daughter of the Moon wasn't supposed to be this vulnerable!

Amidst the embrace, the door flung open. Alina shrieked. Elise and I tightened our hold around our little sister. It didn't matter who'd arrived. Even Nurse Nookes took pity on Alina.

"Sleep. How are my companions supposed to sleep for all

this laughter and crying?" Merile limped in, wrapped into a too-large pristine white cloak with a thick fur lining. The cloak trailed after her, and those rats of hers, all thin fur and thin legs and thin spindly tails, didn't quite know whether to step on it or rush to her sides, and so they bounced from left to right, yapping. To top the already ridiculous entrance, the rats wore coats that matched with her cloak. They were another garish set of gifts from her seed, no doubt about that.

Elise cast an acrid glare at the intruders, and I did likewise. Merile had to understand that the world couldn't always re-volve around her, even if she'd been caught experimenting with dusk, even if that had resulted in a sprained ankle and a limp that wouldn't quite heal. Merile halted, realizing it wasn't just Elise and me in the room, but also little Alina. The prob-lem with acting older than you are, I've been told, is when you misjudge a situation, you end up acting like a fool.

"Dear Merile," Elise said sweetly, but anyone who's ever tasted Nurse Nookes's concoctions knows that syrupy tones often hide a bitter aftertaste. She gently guided Alina around, so that our little sister could see that it was only Merile who'd arrived, not anything one should be afraid of. Unless one counted the fashion disaster the cloak was, too big, too white for someone of Merile's dark complexion. "Would you be so kind as to take Alina back to her room?"

Merile squatted down to pick up one of her rats, and cooed at it. The other one—sure, she repeats the names often enough, but I have long ago decided not to encourage her in this unhealthy affection she feels toward them—rose to its hind legs to lean against her. "I . . ."

Merile struggled so badly to say something coherent that little Alina managed to recover before her. She wiped the tears from the corners of her eyes with the back of her hand and sniffed. "Would you, Merile?"

Merile cradled the rat against her chest. She stared adoringly down at the pile of steel gray legs and the whipping tip of the tail. Her brown face lit up with her smile. "I just might. Bedtime. It was bedtime for Rafa and Mufu already an hour ago."

"Merile!" I stared at her with my eyes about to burst out from the sockets. I swear, dear Notes, sometimes she acts as though her rats were more important to her than her little sister. Can you believe that!

Merile shrugged as if nothing whatsoever under the Moon could affect her as long as she had her rats. But Alina's eyes shone, and not with tears. She wavered a step toward Merile. The brown rat bounced to greet her. She giggled. "Can I help you tuck them into their beds?"

Merile placed the gray rat down and strolled—that is, attempted to stroll despite her limp—to Alina. Though five years older, she's only a head taller than her. Perhaps that's the reason why Alina doesn't find Merile that intimidating—even when Merile acts like she did tonight. "Perhaps. Let me think about it."

"Thank you!" Alina swooped the brown rat up, and it proceeded to lick her face with gusto. Its thin-skinned ears flopped as though she tasted particularly fine. "Oh, you're so silly, Rafa!"

"Isn't she a silly dog? Oh, yes she is! My precious, silly little friend."

And in an eyeblink, Merile and Alina were both completely immersed in scratching and praising the rats. Elise rolled her eyes at me.

I mouthed back at her, "I know."

It took a precious amount of petting and cooing before Merile and Alina were done with the rats. When Merile finally picked the brown rat from Alina and seemed satisfied enough to actually leave, we got yet another visitor.

"Good evening, Daughters of the Moon." And at that moment, when we heard the serene voice, every single one of us halted what we were doing and turned as one to meet our honored eldest sister.

Celestia glided in, every step immensely graceful and equal in length. Dressed in a white gown embroidered with dove pearls, with a mink sash wrapped around her shoulders, she was as regal as ever. Her skin was so fair, almost translucent, her hair so pale, as if spun from silver. A platinum diadem with dove pearls rested on her steep forehead. Her narrow nose divided her face into two symmetrical halves. Her ocean blue eyes . . . They bore a dreamy glow.

I could but stare at her, for she is everything that I'm not. When she steps into a room, everyone will turn to look at her, hearken their ears to hear her precious words, bask in her glorious presence. For she is the empress-to-be, the very promise of prosperity and peace. But tonight, as I admired her, I wondered, had she always radiated such warmth, or was Elise right in her speculations? Dear Notes, I certainly wish she is!

"What is this about?" Celestia tilted her head slightly as though finding her little sisters up well past their bedtime intrigued rather than annoyed her.

I hurried to reclaim the peacock from the tile stove's sill. I'm not sure why I did so, but it seemed important to show rather than tell, to bring the mechanical creature to life, for that was what it had been created for.

But it was Elise who spoke. "Poor little Alina is afraid of the thing."

Merile, her arm wrapped around Alina either for support or for comfort, looked like she might say something. But Celestia lifted a forefinger to her red, red lips. She glided to me—or to the peacock—like a down feather drifts in a winter breeze.

"I will take it then," she said, cupping her palms. She wore long kid gloves. Her arms were svelte, her fingers slim and nimble.

For some reason I still can't figure out, I hesitated to let go of Alina's name day gift. It didn't feel right to part with it, though it wasn't mine to begin with.

"Would you be so kind?" Alina asked, as though Celestia was doing her a favor. Merile's rats gazed up at her, too. Though animals don't like automatons in general either, they seemed perplexed by my little sister's eagerness to rid herself of something that was both beautiful and unique.

Celestia smiled in a hazy, almost distant way. Yes, there was something truly different in that smile compared to the ones with which she'd favored us earlier. Was it one of a woman who'd fallen in love, who'd kissed a man she found to her liking? Perhaps I'd find this out soon myself. She said, "You will never have to see it again."

Alina squealed with joy, and I had no choice but to hand the peacock over to Celestia. Without further words or ceremony, she slipped it into her evening bag. "Merile, would you see Alina to her room?"

And so it was that Merile led Alina out of the room, and along with them went the rats, bouncing to avoid contact with the cold floor tiles. We all, Celestia included, gazed after them. For a moment I thought she might shake her head, but that she didn't do. Instead she turned to Elise and said, "Are you ready to go? The carriage is waiting for us."

This was my cue to exit, and that I did, though Celestia hadn't really said anything to me. It was as if I didn't really exist, as if my presence didn't matter to her. I must admit that this was a most peculiar feeling, something I must have no doubt only imagined.

Dear Notes, this is everything of relevance that came to pass today. Some things mightn't make much sense, but I can't be bothered to think of them now. For I have many reasons to be happy. Happy, happy, happy! I think I'll stop writing now and start dreaming of K.

For one day soon there will be kisses and caresses.

Chapter 4

Elise

As I undress in the dim-lit room, a thought crosses my mind. I never asked to be born a Daughter of the Moon, to be placed on a pedestal, to be admired as pristine and white. But that's a lame excuse. The poor never asked to be hungry and cold either.

Ever since I met my love, I knew I had to change. I knew it to be true like a toddler who knows that her first wavering steps are just the beginning, like a child who realizes that letters form words that unfold into countless stories, like a sailor who upon stepping on a foreign shore realizes that even if he were to ever return home, it wouldn't be the same place he left behind.

"Shawl," Lily, my governess, hums as she holds her right arm out for me. Hers is a voice that comforts me, the buzzing of bees collecting honey.

I swirl and unwrap the fur-trimmed cashmere from around my shoulders. And although the fair hair on my arms jumps up instantly, I fold it on her arms. It's chilly in this room that isn't mine, but which I have started to think of as belonging to me. Hidden somewhere under the vast garden, reachable only by servants' corridors—no one will see me enter or leave. There's no stove here, no fireplace, only a few candles of the rougher sort on the rickety table accompanied by two equally forgotten chairs. The air smells of tallow and burning hair.

"Gloves." Lily's tune veers toward the melancholy paths that I have grown so accustomed to. Perhaps it was as much my darker moods as it was her family's tragedy that shaped her such as she is. A woman twice my age. Wiry, but kind. Though she has been told to keep her gaze down her whole life, her angular chin always points up. Her gaze is sharp, and she sees everything. Sometimes this frightens me a little.

I pull off my white satin gloves, first the left one, then the right. I never complained of how unhappy I felt, but it could hardly have escaped my governess. For the longest time, I tried to bury my darker feelings and feign that I only knew joy. For everyone wanted to see and know the sparkling, giggling Elise. And so I practiced before my mirrors how to hide my anxiety until no one, not even dear Sibs, could see through the mask I had so carefully crafted.

"The dress."

Lily and I go through this ritual every night, but lately it has meant more to me. One garment, now one button at a time, I cease to be an obsolete leftover from an age that's about to come to an end. It's all because of him, the captain of my heart.

The undusted, crooked floorboards creak as I step out of the dress, the white chiffon creation draped to resemble a midsummer rose in bloom. Lily swoops the dress up and pauses her humming. "What shall I do with this one?"

Without hesitation I answer, "Sell it and donate the funds for the cause."

Lily nods, her lips pressing into a timid smile. The cause, whatever it turns out to be in the end, is important to her, too. She was born into a noble bloodline, but her family lost its fortune. At ten, she was sent away and brought up to serve. To me, she's a servant only in name. She's my confidante.

"Jewelry."

Dressed only in my silk undergarments, I hold my hair bundled atop my head. Lily unclips the necklace with one practiced move. The dove pearls and diamonds shine in the flickering light, as if to mock me for wanting to leave my privileged life behind. If it were up to me, I would be very glad to never see the wretched thing again. But as it is, I'm already tiptoeing on thin ice.

Lily's beady eyes glint with longing, anger even, as she holds the glittering arc of the necklace. She doesn't yearn to wear such once more, doesn't grieve after her lost life, of that I'm sure. She dreams of a world where people are equal and not burdened by their parents' mistakes. "And this one?"

I don't know what to say, and so I stroll to the closest chair. I pick up the simple dress folded there. Thin black and blue stripes with a wild floral pattern run down the front of the dress. The frayed hem has worn smooth. The smell of root cellar fills my nostrils. I was nervous the first time I abandoned white in favor of the colors of my people. I'm more nervous now. "I . . ."

Lily pads to stand behind me, so close that I feel her breath against my shoulder blades. She hums an encouraging little tune. She means well, but . . .

"Please stop." I clutch the dress against my chest. Every lie I tell to Sibs adds more weight on my shoulders. She suspects already that I'm up to something more than a simple romance, and it's just a matter of time until I plunge through the shards into a coldness that will never leave my bones. "I can't do it."

Lily clicks her tongue, in sympathy I hope, for she has never disapproved of me. Not even when I led a life of leisure, wasting what could have been cherished. The veins on her sinewy arms seem more pronounced as she places the necklace on the table. She straightens it out of old habit.

As I step into the simple dress, I shiver, but not from cold. A Daughter of the Moon should only ever wear white. That's her right. That's her duty. If my celestial father could see me now, he might curse me or merely laugh at me. But he can't, and he won't. I can't go to where I need to go as a Daughter of the Moon.

"Do you know where he'll take me tonight?" I ask Lily. I never know the destination my love has in mind beforehand, but I suspect Lily knows the details. Every time he shows me more. I feel akin to a novice in a cloister who is tested to see if she's really devoted enough to take the vows. Perhaps my love and Lily still doubt my commitment to the cause or fear my tongue might slip. I can only continue to strive to show my worth to them.

"All in good time," Lily replies.

Though I have practiced, I'm still slow at dressing on my own. Who could believe two full-length sleeves and a few buttons can pose such a challenge to me? It embarrasses me how useless I was. Still am. The captain of my heart, he knows this, and yet he loves me.

"How do I look?" I ask as I finally finish fumbling with the dress.

"Hmh..." Lily eyes me from head to toe. She pulls my sleeves straight and nods at the buttons I had forgotten to do. I'm not used to long sleeves. "The cause has come to rely on your contribution."

I lick my lips and taste tallow. I think of those who would be glad of these candles, who must live in darkness through the cruel winter months because they need their meager coins for rye bread and salted herring. The necklace, lounging lazily on the table, dares to glitter.

How many mouths could one feed with its cost? Many. So many, and I wouldn't even miss it. There would be a new one to replace it before too long. Some nobleman would send one as a token of love that would never be. Or worse, a poor town might spend what they can't afford to send me a gift to gain my favor. All the same, both useless acts doomed to fail. I don't want an aristocratic lover. Political favors are not for me to grant.

"There won't be more if I get caught," I reply at last. This isn't about the superstition that I should look after the beads gifted to me. No, not about that. If Celestia or my mother or anyone else were to ever learn that I conspire to change the empire, I would . . . I have often thought of it. I would be sentenced to death or exile. And yet, I have never felt more alive than I do now.

"Sell the dress"—I nudge my fine slippers off my feet and step into the borrowed sabots—"Sell the shoes. Sell the shawl and gloves. But we must find some other way to milk money from the empire than selling my jewelry."

Lily nods, the veins on her neck tight and taut. I think that sometimes she fears I'm not fully dedicated. That this is just a phase for me.

But it's not. I—my kind—can't exist with the cause. But I can't exist without it anymore. It has brought an end to my ennui. It fuels me and gives my existence a purpose.

I button my sleeves around my wrists. It's time to become what I was meant to be.

A knock on the door—short and short, long and short—means that my love is here at last. I give my woolen scarf one last tug. Tied tight under my chin, the poppy petals shift, but the scarf itself won't budge. Good. For if my true identity were revealed, if I were caught unprotected outside the palace grounds . . . How curious it is that I'm risking so much, and both sides would wish ill for me if they knew.

Lily strides to slide off the bolt. Her low heels clack against the floorboards. The bolt squeals. These sounds, no matter how normal, itch my nerves. Yet at the same time my heart pangs with indecipherable joy. Even a moment apart from my love feels too much for me to bear. A day is pure torture.

The door opens, and I see my love at last.

Captain Janlav is handsome, though he's no longer dressed in his midnight blue uniform with silver epaulets and gleaming crescent buttons. A black newsboy hat, with flaps tied under his strong chin, hides his loosened topknot and the shaved sides of his head. He has pulled up the collar of his factory-woven coat. It has a stained, murky brown hem, and it stinks of wet lambs. A knitted red scarf bulges out from the front. He wears workman's leather gloves, likewise red. He doesn't look at all like an imperial soldier, which is good. A disguise is almost as important to him as it is to me.

My love meets my gaze from across the room, and a ripple of tingles runs through my body. His brown eyes—the shade of young pines—are bright and full of love. As he smiles at me, his glorious brown moustache rises with the curve of his lips. His is uniquely the boyish mischief mixed with a grown man's seriousness.

"Are you ready?" he asks with a lopsided grin, as if he were truly a railway man courting a factory girl.

I cant my head in a somewhat coquettish fashion before I can stop myself. He shouldn't have needed to even ask. I will follow him wherever he leads me. For ever since our gazes met at Alina's name day ball three months ago, I knew, I simply knew he was the one. My destiny.

"I am," I reply, even as I dash to him. I fling my arms around his neck and rise on my toes. Our lips touch, and we breathe the same air. But only shortly, for romantics come later. First we shall make the world a better place.

As we leave the room, he doesn't say where he's taking me, and I don't ask. I simply follow behind him, never glancing back. It drizzles in the tunnels, and I can't keep track of the turns. We are somewhere under the palace garden, in the tunnels between the canals. That is all I know.

Though this isn't my first time in the tunnels, I would get lost without my love, for we always take a different route, always go to a different destination. It's warmer here than outside, and yet my toes go numb in the slightly-too-small sabots. Algae and mold cling to the rough walls. My eyes water and nose dribbles. My sisters and I, we have always known of the existence of these tunnels, but not about their true extent. I suspect my sisters don't know the truth about many things, my younger sisters even less.

I fell in love with my captain upon first laying eyes on him. In the beginning, when our romance was merely budding, we slipped out of concerts and balls, into balconies and courtyards, just to talk and gaze at the stars. Gradually we grew bolder. We sneaked into the forgotten parts of the garden and sought shelter from abandoned pavilions. He could see straight into my lonely heart, how I longed to be more than beautiful, how I yearned to do more than just exist, to see what lay behind the palace grounds. He listened to me, and then after a month or so, on one starlit night, he promised to show me the world as it truly was. And though he warned me that there would be no turning back, I didn't hesitate.

The very next night he kept his word.

The orphanage was located at what can only be called the bad part of this city. There decaying houses leaned against each other, leaving between them gaps so narrow that we could barely walk side by side. The lanes were aflood with mud and offal. He would have carried me the whole way, but I refused. That would have gathered too much attention.

My love had smuggled a breadbasket with him, throwaway pieces from the palace. Someone in the kitchen, a scullery maid or boy, had collected them during the week. Some pieces had a bite nibbled out, others sauce stains. I was embarrassed of that. Had I only asked I could have brought a cartful of loaves fresh out of the oven!

At the rusting gates of the orphanage a country gagargi greeted us. He didn't recognize either one of us, disguised as we were as a working-class couple. He led us into the unlit house, there to meet the children.

The orphanage was like no other institution I have ever visited. Instead of timidly smiling children in starched black shirts and dresses, this house was full of scrawny creatures that I couldn't tell apart from each other. With heads shaved bare to prevent vermin, with big staring eyes and hollow cheeks, with stick arms and legs poking out from the sheets and blankets they had drawn over their bent shoulders, they didn't look like children at all, but prisoners most poorly handled. Creatures who wouldn't live long enough to name themselves, for their souls to anchor to their bodies.

But there, in a hall with a low ceiling, at the end of a wobbly table, an equally scrawny woman stood behind a cracked ceramic pot filled with watery beetroot soup. As the children sat on the rickety benches, the country gagargi read a sermon. *All who can should share. So be praised the Moon.* I wondered then, had my family forgotten something along the way? Something very important? Why did we live apart from our people in a palace guarded by soldiers? Why did we waste so much when others had next to nothing?

The scrawny woman motioned my love and me to come and help her. At first I hesitated, but my love, he obeyed at once. As he revealed the contents of his basket, the children cheered and the woman cried. It was the first time in my life that I did something good. I swore then it wouldn't be my last.

"Stop," my love whispers.

I chastise myself for getting so lost in my thoughts. He holds his fist up, unable to shake off his military habits even when he pretends to be someone else than a man devoted to serve the empire.

I hear it then, too. Faint, regular thumps from right above us. Faded note of a horn. My heart beats faster, and the air, colder now, pinches my nostrils. We are in a tunnel much narrower than those right under the palace. How far have we come already? How far is there still left to go? When my love escorts me to the opera or theater, we can sneak out together, and all there will be is a scandal of a Daughter of the Moon embarking upon a fling. But now that we are both disguised, the guards would shoot us before asking for our names.

"Do not fear." My love squeezes my hand and presses a kiss

on my forehead. "It's just the guard change at the gates. Now I know where everyone is."

He continues to lead the way. I follow my love, him who opened my eyes and showed me how the people of our empire really fare. Though I step lightly, echoes follow me. Echoes always follow me. The age of my kind is running out. Soon I'll be but an echo, too.

I refuse to feel pity for myself. It's a terrible burden to know too much, and I have known too much for years. I was younger than Alina now is when I first realized that under the glitter the world is but a dark place. Perhaps my sister has realized this, too. Perhaps the visions that haunt her are but reality. I should talk to her and find out. I will talk to her.

The tunnel narrows even more, and I must fall behind my love. I seek comfort from the wideness of his shoulders, his steady gait. He must have sensed this, for he glances over his shoulder and smiles reassuringly. "Almost there."

A part of me doesn't even care where he's leading me. I trust him, and Lily trusts him, too. And I trust her. After my visit to the orphanage, I asked her to tell me what really went on in my mother's empire. She did so, honestly and without protecting my sensibilities. She told me that while we danced and feasted, the people worked long, hard days and starved. Starved as thanks for their servitude, and that hadn't escaped the people either.

My love halts before an iron-reinforced door. The metal seeps coldness; I can feel it drifting past him. Though I hearken my senses, I can't hear any sounds, hints of what awaits us.

My love pulls out a jingling key ring from inside his coat. "Ready?"

Suddenly, despite all my apparent altruism and determination, I'm not sure. My love has taken me to many desolate places. Places where sounds are harsh and loud, where there's no escaping the stink of offal and sweat and dust and tar and crushed bone. Places where families are broken apart, to never see each other again, orphanages and workhouses. Hospitals, where wounded soldiers are out of sight, out of mind. Proud men sobbing in crammed rooms, on filthy straw mattresses, unable to serve the empire, simply waiting to die.

"Elise?" The brightness of my love's voice brings me back, into the tunnel, before the iron-bound door. He has turned the key in the lock already. He is only waiting for me. "Are you ready?"

I tug my scarf tighter. I secure my red mittens under my coat sleeves. Wherever he is leading me, I will follow, no matter how the reality may frighten me. "Yes."

We step through the door.

The stink of urine assaults us. It's dim in the room, which has pale blue walls and a bare concrete floor. I blink to prevent my eyes from watering as Janlav locks the door behind us. It feels to me as if we are being watched.

Janlav secures the key ring back inside his coat. He takes hold of my hand. "Come."

I can't make myself move. For I can see that we aren't actually in a room, but in a short corridor. Steep stairs lead out into the night, but even the icy wind can't chase away the incredibly strong stink of urine. Two rooms flank the corridor. In the doorway to our right, an old woman clutches a shawl around her bony shoulders.

Janlav follows my gaze. But rather than tensing, he smiles at the woman. As he leads me past her, he nods at her. "Evening, little mother."

The old woman smirks at us. Her cheeks are red either from the cold or liquor. "Evening, young lovers."

I turn my gaze down as if embarrassed. She has no idea of who I am or that the door we closed hides a tunnel that goes all the way from the palace to a . . . public latrine. She just thinks that my love and I are a young couple embarked on mischief that might result in babies. Though that we aren't—Celestia has yet to announce the name of her first lover.

Resisting the urge to laugh at the absurdness of it, I climb up the stairs, into the night that awaits us.

The main street stretches before us, as empty as I have ever seen it. It's so late that not many carriages or carts brave the low temperatures. Wind swirls light snow above the wide flag-stones and iron tracks of the trolleys. The air is full of pinprick flakes, and soon my cheeks and nose glow red.

"Is that the railway station?" I ask, unable to believe my eyes, that the tunnels could really lead this far.

"It is."

The railway station stands right before us, an imposing building with an elaborate stucco facade, complete with carvings honoring my father. I glance at the sky, all too aware of how I'm betraying my sacred family. But the night is cloudy, and I can't catch even a glimpse of my father. I pray this means that he can't see me either.

"Come," my love urges.

My sabots slip on the frozen pavement as he leads me toward the station. Are we going to leave by train? Do trains still go this late? Will we make it back in time, before I'm missed? A thousand questions bud in my mind, but I can't ask them, lest I break my disguise.

We don't enter the railway station, but halt at the trolley

stop before it. It's nothing more than a slightly wider stretch of pavement with a sign hanging from an iron arch and a pen made of planks painted gray. The pen is full already, full of people wrapped up from head to toe in factory-woven coats and shawls and blankets. A few sport lamb furs, tattered things showing decades of stains. My love greets these people with a nod. They nod back at him. I don't know what to do, but it doesn't matter. When I'm with him, I belong everywhere.

"Are we going to take a trolley?" The mere thought of doing so sends my heart pounding. Whenever I travel farther than I can walk, it's either with the imperial train or in a comfortable carriage with a platoon of soldiers escorting me.

My love draws me into an embrace that smells of wood smoke and cigarettes. He places his chin on my shoulder, and I can feel his warm breath through the floral scarf shielding my cheeks. "I love you."

I cling to him more desperately than I care to admit. The night around us is cold, but at that moment it doesn't matter. He loves me, and I love him.

It's a new experience for me to wait for the trolley. For a Daughter of the Moon, everything always happens at once. When I'm her, I don't wait—others wait for me. But I'm not myself tonight.

More people gather at the trolley stop. A group of railway men huddle right next to us. The biggest and burliest of them sips from a dented flask and offers it to my love. "Care to wager a bet, man? I bet that on a night like this the imperial family drinks mulled wine as they roast deer before a roaring fire. All wrapped in their nice white furs, sipping nice hot drinks, while we ordinary people chill our arses off."

I tense and cringe despite myself. Though the railway man

masks his displeasure with jokes, the undercurrent of anger runs so strong that eventually it will flood. For he's right, even as ashamed as I am to admit that.

My love, he just chuckles, declining the flask with a jovial shake of his head. When he speaks, his voice is different from what I know. Rough around the edges, as if he, too, worked at the railways, day after day. "You've got the wrong man. I'm not much of a betting man."

The railway man shrugs. He sways toward us and halts right before me. He peers down at me, as if trying to see what my scarf hides. "What do you think, young lass?"

"Ah, don't tease her." Janlav nudges him on the shoulder, just a friendly reminder that I'm with him, not someone to be bothered with unwanted attention. "My love, she's a shy one."

The railway man snorts, mucus frosting under his nose. His bushy beard glistens with snowflakes. His breath smells of rye liquor. "What sort of rebels are we if we don't listen to what our little misses have to say?"

He squats down and stares at me with such unrelenting interest that I can't bring myself to turn my face away. How does he see me? As I am or as I pretend to be?

Every day I see my face a thousand times in the mirrors scattered around the palace. My skin is pale as porcelain, kept more so by cream and powder. My cheeks are freckled, stubbornly so. My eyes are gray, rimmed by blackened lashes. Mine isn't a face that belongs to a factory girl.

Be that as it may, I can but try. I lift my chin up and meet the man's stare, not with defiance, but with a smile as luminous as a flame first summoned to life. I should be afraid. But I like this world, the world without ranks. Where people are what they are and nothing more or less. I say, "The cause is right.

The cause is just. That is what I think."

In my ears, my trained voice is akin to a nightingale's song. True enough, the railway man staggers up as if I had cursed at him. I hold my breath. Behind me, Janlav's pose has changed. He's a soldier dressed in plain clothes now.

A screech of metal on metal tears through the night. Neighs and clicking of iron-shod hooves scatter against the ice-laced flagstones. The people crammed into the pen swarm out. I dash to my love before I realize it's just the trolley arriving.

The trolley draws to a halt, and people surround us. The railway man still stares at me in wonder, for he hasn't—I know it for sure—ever before seen or heard one like me.

"You." The railway man points a trembling finger squarely at my love's chest. "You are one very lucky man. Never let go of her. Never let her go."

My love's pose eases. He swoops an arm around my waist and pulls me against him. I shiver out of sheer exhilaration of being so close to him. "Never! I swear as the Moon is my witness. I will never let go of her."

The railway man chuckles, and then he's already boarding the trolley. He pushes people around him aside to make space for us. "Hop in, friends!"

My love smiles wildly at him, and we board the trolley. As the trolley jerks onward, my love whispers in my ear, "You did good."

I don't reply a word. I truly am one amongst many. This is the future.

It's silent in the trolley, almost as if we were in a church, listening to a gagargi speak. As the trolley rattles over the stone bridge that arches over the Navna River, I stare through the window fogged by the breath of dozens of people. The train bridge runs alongside this bridge, but no locomotive steams through the night. Was it just this spring when I leaned out of the imperial train's window, so overjoyed to arrive in the Summer City? This bridge was then crammed with people waving white handkerchiefs at us.

"Or perhaps it was just pieces of cloth, ripped from old sheets and shirts," I mutter under my breath before I can stop myself.

The trolley screeches as it changes tracks. The people gripping the poles or holding on to each other sway. My love bumps into me, but not by accident. "What was that you said?"

"Oh, nothing important," I say as I realize something I was too blind to see earlier. All the people in the trolley wear red gloves or mittens.

The trolley rattles through the city for a good hour or so before it draws to a halt before a massive warehouse. The red-brown bricks bear a white veil. Snow rests on the slanted roof.

Sensing that I can't place us on the map, my love says, "We are at the train depot."

People disembark the trolley in an orderly, even jolly manner. The current carries my love and me out, toward the sliding doors that yawn wide open.

"Stay close." My love squeezes my hand.

"I will," I reply, though he wouldn't have needed to remind me. Even if he isn't wearing the imperial uniform, he radiates such confidence, bears such an air of command around him, that people shuffle out of our way without even noticing that they are doing so. I clutch his hand as people close in behind us. For if I were to lose him, I would never find him again in this crowd, and I might not be able to navigate my way back to the Summer Palace without risking revealing my identity.

The train depot is a vast steel structure with a large lattice of windows as a ceiling. Thin snow covers the glass panes, piled by wind into waves. Huge lanterns hang from the iron bars spanning across the whole hall. The tiny lights flicker, too weak to chase away this many shadows. I think they are powered by chicken souls, but it might be another cheap soul that's in use.

"At least it's warm here." A man in a peasant's baggy shirt nudges his mate with his elbow. His shirt is cinched at the waist with a leather belt re-holed too many times. "Eh?"

"Now, if there only were a piece of bread to be had, then we'd know what it feels like to live in the palace!"

I glue my gaze down, on the oil-stained concrete. If these two men only knew how much goes to waste in the palace! We nibble and sample and taste for fun, only to send away practically untouched plates because some minor detail didn't quite please us. Or because we have changed our minds about what we want for breakfast or lunch or brunch or dinner. I can't plead innocence, having committed those crimes too many times to count. My sisters and I, we are as guilty as any who dwell in the world that these men can't even imagine.

Because I gaze down, I happen to lock eyes with an elderly woman whose head comes only up to my knees; she's standing in a longitudinal depression that runs all the way to the end of the hall. A railway track, I realize. I stare back at the woman, impressed by her boldness. People don't often meet my eyes, not when I'm a Daughter of the Moon. The woman presses her fist tight against her heart. She, too, wears a red mitten.

I repeat the gesture, though I don't know what it means. The gloves and mittens and rags around hands, they must signify something. But what, I can only guess. All these people in the train depot, they are connected by the same concerns and goals. And there are enough of them, in the small towns and cities, spread across the whole empire, to make a difference at last.

"Come."

I let my love lead me farther into the hall, where the crowd gets thicker and louder. Even the railway depressions are packed with people. Railroad workers in their loose trousers and boots that have seen too many feet, faces black with oil and coal, stuck in permanent grimaces carved by the harsh winters. There's militia, too, men whose coats and trousers bear silver stripes, huddling in groups of two and three, mainly footmen. Women stand proud alongside these men, floral scarves tied around their heads, with furs on their shoulders, lamb and fox and wolf, with aprons peeking from under their long coats. Some don't have coats, but many dresses layered for warmth. There are too many children to count, the scruffy sort that live on the streets.

A thought occurs to me, one that I try to push aside, but that's too sharp for me to touch. These pits with rails, they are full of people, thousand-eyed trains. Smoke, it's from their breath. The hoots, from their mouths. And once these trains roll into motion, they will be unstoppable.

I hear a snippet of conversation, but can't pinpoint the person talking. The words are no less impactful. "How can the Moon watch over us when the empire has tripled in size? Perhaps he simply doesn't see our plight. Perhaps that's why he lets us suffer."

I glance up out of reflex. A thicker layer of snow covers the ceiling now. I can't see out through the windows, and ask my father if it's really him who has failed our people, or only my family.

I stumble in my sabots; my toes are solidly frozen. A flicker of concern crosses my love's proud forehead, and he guides me toward the side of the hall, where the pressure of the crowd isn't as intense. Once there, he places himself firmly behind me, wraps his arms around me. "This is far enough, I think."

I smile despite myself. No matter what will happen in this world, with him I will be safe. I'm privileged in more than one way. I plant a kiss on his clean-shaven chin.

But his attention is elsewhere. He's craning over the crowd, looking intently toward the back of the hall. Ah, there, a narrow stairway leads from the ground level to what must be the foreman's office. Men with shoulders so wide that they must no doubt walk through doors sideways stand guard at the bottom of the stairs and on the platform midway up. They remind me of the railway man I talked with earlier. So full of uncontrolled anger and power. Ready to beat even metal into submission.

Whatever is going to happen tonight, I realize, is going to take place at the platform. For gradually everyone in the crowd turns to stare in that direction. I chew the inside of my lips as my heart pounds faster, with vigor. This is altogether different from the other places my love has taken me. This is a gathering of unhappy souls, of people who yearn for change. People like me. And people not at all like me. I want to know one thing above everything else. Whom are we waiting to see? Whom are we waiting to hear speak?

I glance over my shoulder at Janlav. He must have known what I'm about to ask, but he just places his red-gloved hand against my heart. I place my red-mittened hand atop his. He won't tell me. He wants me to listen to my heart.

At last, the door of the foreman's office slowly opens. I rise on my toes to catch the first glimpse of the person all these people have come to hear speak. The sabots press painfully against my toes, and though my ankles threaten to twist, I rise higher. I want to know this person's name, for he or she is the one to whom I must offer my help if I'm to change this empire for the better.

A man emerges through the doorway and halts at the first step of the iron staircase. He is tall and his dark hair is braided. He wears the black robes of a gagargi. I know this man, though his presence here is very much impossible. He's a man of the empire as much as I'm its daughter.

But I'm not mistaken, for the crowd knows him too.

"Prataslav! Prataslav!" The rising roar slams breath from my lungs. The crowd punches their right fists in the air, and above their heads red spreads like blood spilled. "Our great Gagargi Prataslav. The gagargi of the people!"

I can't say his name, for my tongue has gone numb; not even as I feel my love's chest expand, hear his voice joining the cheer. I was expecting the leader of the insurgence to be of high position, one of the generals perhaps, or a high-ranking court official. Never even in my darkest dreams did I imagine him to be Gagargi Prataslav.

Gagargi Prataslav, my mother's closest advisor, openly placing himself against the empire. This is as pure a treason as can ever be. It's almost worse than what I'm up to, for I'm only the second daughter!

A gust of warmth touches my left cheek. I flinch before I realize it's just my love about to whisper in my ear. "You are surprised?"

I don't dare to let him see my expression. For I'm shocked more than surprised. I was ready to offer my help for the insurgence movement. But now that I know that it's led by Gagargi Prataslav... There's something odd, even frightening about him. Both Alina and Merile openly fear him, and not only because they saw something not meant for their eyes, I suspect. I cautiously study the frenzied crowd. A mere moment earlier, I considered myself a part of it. But now... now I want to run away as fast as my feet can carry me.

Before I can form the words that would surely drive my love away from me, the crowd stills. Even my love stills, forgetting he asked me a question. My gaze is drawn toward the balcony of its own accord. For it's not possible for this many people to be this quiet, this unrelentingly focused, but I swear, I swear I could hear a feather drift, set against the floor. It's that quiet.

"Thank you," Gagargi Prataslav says as he floats down the steps to the platform, or that's how it seems. His black robes hide the movement of his legs, and his boots don't make a sound. Apart from his voice, nothing exists. "Thank you for gathering here to hear what a man has to say to his equals."

My jaw slackens as the numbness of my tongue spreads through my body. For him to act so boldly, so openly to step down from his podium... Myself, I can imagine living a life much simpler, but he's supposed to be the sacred messenger of the Moon!

With an effort that cramps my cold-tensed muscles, I manage to crane my neck and glance at the ceiling. My father can't see us. Not with the snowfall thickening. Not with all the windows being just dark panes of dirty glass tonight.

Gagargi Prataslav halts exactly in the middle of the narrow

platform and spreads his arms wide. His black sleeves are like the wings of a crow, the bearer of bad news and ill tidings. He leans toward the crowd, toward us, as he always does. Though he's on the platform, he's still too close for comfort. His gaze searches the crowd, and he smiles to himself as if he knew the name and lineage of everyone present. "I know why you have come here tonight."

And it's as if he's speaking to me! My urge to flee strengthens, and I stumble backward, tread on my love's toes. The gagargi can't know I'm present. He mustn't learn that I'm here. For if he did . . .

"The time of change is upon us. Soon we will all be what we were meant to be, regardless of our birth and origin."

The crowd listens to the gagargi's words in utter silence, with faces carved from stone. No eye blinks. No nostril flares. I have never witnessed such before. Not even in the churches during the holiest of ceremonies devoted to my father. Always, always someone has coughed in his fist or a baby has burst into tears. But now . . . even the unsteady beat of my heart is too loud in the confines of my shrinking ribcage.

"Very soon," Gagargi Prataslav says, and lifts his right hand in the air, extends his long, bony forefinger. He, too, wears red gloves. His voice is low and mellow, and everyone in the hall must surely strain their ears to hear the words. "The Great Thinking Machine will make everyone equal."

The machine? I have just enough time for that one frightening thought.

"Aya!" The crowd bursts into a reply so strong that it feels as if the very air were vibrating. My love joins the ear-shattering chorus. People lift their right fists in the air again, and the sea of red spreads over them. I wonder—wherever this thought came from—if eventually we are all going to drown in our own blood. "Aya! Aya, at last!"

I frown in open puzzlement. The crowd knows more than I do. What does the gagargi's machine have to do with anything? How can the people know more than I, who have seen the thing with my own eyes? I who know what it requires for fuel!

"No more starving children." Gagargi Prataslav's words ring loud and clear, as though every word was produced by a smith's hammer against an anvil. "No more soldiers sent to certain death. The machine knows everything. The machine cares for every single one of us. This is the end of injustice."

Injustice? I shiver despite the multitude of layers hiding my identity. But, yes. My mother thinks her rule just, but that it is not. She has been so focused on expanding the empire that she has forgotten those she is supposed to shelter. She sends men to faraway countries, while their families slave in the fields. And to fund these excursions, she has increased taxes, so that the families have nothing to show for their hard work but debts.

But nothing in this world comes without a price. I have seen the Great Thinking Machine. And though I claimed otherwise to Alina and Merile, it runs on human souls. That's the reason why Mother rejected it. How is the gagargi planning to solve that blasphemy?

"Equality is efficiency." Gagargi Prataslav's gaze brightens as if he were burning with passion inside. And perhaps he is. "No price is too great for such freedom. No price is too great for a better world."

I wonder, do the people know the true price? Perhaps not. How will they react when they find out? Will they ever find out? What is the gagargi's plan?

"The Moon has blessed our cause," the gagargi says, his voice is so enchanting, so mellow. He turns sideways and gestures up the stairs, toward the foreman's office.

A woman in a hooded cloak the color of a cherry sliced open stands in the gaping doorway. She's almost as tall as he is. I can't yet say anything else about her, but she must be of great importance to the gagargi.

The crowd holds their breath once more as the woman descends the stairs. Her movements are ethereal, beyond graceful. The edge of her cloak trails behind her, barely touching the floor.

There's something familiar about the way she moves, commands the space to accommodate her movements. When she takes her place before the gagargi, I'm sure I have seen her before. When the gagargi whispers in her ear, she nods in reply, a curt, imperial gesture. I know her name then, even before she pushes the hood back and reveals her symmetrical face.

"Celestia . . ." I whisper before I can stop myself. What is my sister, the heir to the empire, doing up there, with the gagargi? My neck clicks as I turn to meet the man who brought me here. "Did you know about this?"

The crowd mills about in confusion, and my love's gaze is wide with wonder. He might have known about the gagargi and hidden that from me until tonight, but . . . "No. I swear to the Moon, I didn't. None of us did! But this is wonderful!"

Gagargi Prataslav and Celestia wait as if they had all the time in this world. My sister has a placid, almost dreamy expression on her face. Her silver hair is undecorated, merely curled. She wears a white dress with a high waistline, and white satin gloves envelop her svelte arms. As she places a hand on the railing, Gagargi Prataslav places his on top of hers.

I gasp, but there's not enough air in the hall to fill my clenched lungs. I have suspected for some time already that my sister has a lover. But now it's glaringly obvious. Her first lover is none other than Gagargi Prataslav. And for her to present this man to the common people before announcing her choice in the court . . . I don't know what to think of it. For that matter, I don't know what to think of anything anymore.

The sound is faint, a mere clatter of boots against metal. But it's real, and it comforts me.

A guard has climbed up the stairway to the platform and brought with him a wooden tray. On the tray is a simple glass pitcher filled with dark liquid and an equally simple glass bowl. The guard holds it out before the gagargi. The gagargi picks up the pitcher and raises it over the railing. "Our hands have always been red with the blood we have bled for this empire."

People cheer once more, and I wonder if they ever tire of shouting. If they have lost their mind in consensus. If I'm the only one really thinking of what lies under the surface.

For it's not wine in the pitcher, but thick, clotted blood. I watch as one of the crowd as the gagargi pours the blood into the bowl, for what else can I do? Celestia, she just stares directly ahead of her. As if she really were not present. Or as if she existed only as a shadow in the world beyond this one.

The gagargi lowers the pitcher onto the tray and then accepts the whole tray from the guard. He turns to my sister. "This has not escaped the Moon. Tonight, next to me, stands his eldest, honored Celestia, the empress-to-be."

Celestia turns her head slowly, her whole body. Hers is the most exquisite silhouette; slender, but round at bosom and hips. Her red cloak rests against her white gown, heavier than it should.

"I am here for you," she says, and then ... She sinks her hands into the bowl. "I am one of you."

I gape in utter horror as Celestia raises her hands up in the air. Blood dribbles down her wrists, her arms, onto her dress, onto her pale neck, even onto her face. Her expression doesn't flinch. No, it's utterly serene as she faces the crowd once more.

"Celestia!" The crowd bursts into the loudest of shouts yet. "Prataslav! The age of equality!"

My mouth moves on its own, but no words come out. If I had thought I'd anger my father by wearing peasant clothes in public, Celestia ... she has gone too far. In her scarlet cloak, in her bloodstained dress ... I don't understand the game she is playing. And yet I do. She means to overtake our mother with the help of the gagargi.

Gagargi Prataslav smiles, a self-satisfied smirk, visible for a moment only then gone so fast that I'm not sure I saw right. A thought occurs to me.

Perhaps it's not Celestia who is behind the insurgence. Gagargi Prataslav has already won the heart of the people. With my sister by his side, he will have no trouble gaining the support of the nobles. Dizzy, I seek support from the man I thought I loved.

For a long time I had known that the time of my kind was coming to an end. Now I know this will happen very, very soon indeed.

Chapter 5

Celestia

It is the eve of the winter solstice. The tiny, cobwebbed windows bar the way in for the Moon's light. The ceiling is low, the thick roof beams deeply grained. I lie on a bed, next to a man who smells of incense and musk, feral. Furs and sheets shelter us from the cold, but neither are white. I am not sure where I am or why I am here. I am sure of only two things.

In mere hours, when the clock strikes twelve, I will claim my place as the Crescent Empress. And mere moments ago, I let a man touch me for the very first time. And that . . .

I rise to lean on my elbows, away from the body that presses against mine. A thousand rules bind a Daughter of the Moon, a thousand ceremonies await her. By doing what I have done, I have skipped one of the most important ones. "The ceremony . . ."

"Ah, Celestia." His voice is but a quiet growl, a thunder rolling in the distance. "Do you not remember? There is no need for one. No need to announce your lover to the court, for your mother to witness the consummation, for the gathered gagargis and nobles to watch me examine the stains on the sheets and preach prophesies that may or may not come true. In your empire, there is no need for such useless, ancient antics."

My empire. Yes, I am the oldest, and it is mine by birthright. Mother, may she live a long life in her exile-to-come, under her guidance the empire has expanded, but at a terrible price. In the coming revolution, hers will not be the winning side. Mine will be.

"What the Crescent Empire needs is the empress and her sacred gagargis working together for the better of their people. There cannot be a more blessed union than ours."

But for a moment, I struggle to even remember his name. He speaks as if I know him. Which must be true, for it isn't in my nature to lose my virtue to a complete stranger.

"Come closer." The bed creaks as he shifts to sit with his back against the headboard. He draws a sheet with him, either to keep him warm or to shelter me from seeing that which has already been inside me. "Lay your head on my lap."

I roll over to accommodate to this, for it would be silly indeed of me to refuse this request that is so innocent in the light of what we have just done. It is then that I see his pale, bearded face. My eyes lock with the gaze so dark and intense that I can't believe that I ever forgot his name.

"You need not worry." Gagargi Prataslav smiles at me, and it is as if he knew every thought that has ever crossed my mind. He brushes a lock of hair behind my left ear. He caresses my cheeks with his long, bony fingers.

Though unfathomable sadness buds in the pit of my stomach, I refuse to cry. An empress never cries. For a ruler's best weapon is her mind, a machinery that must keep on working even in the most dire of circumstances. Though I am not made of metal, tears may dull the cogs and wheels. I swallow the lump swelling in my throat, and think and analyze.

"You wanted it," the gagargi says, drawing a circle on my

forehead. His skin is rough against mine, that of an artisan who works with metal. I try to remember what his touch felt like earlier.

Lovers do intimate things together. But I can't remember any that I may or may not have done with the gagargi. When I was with him—this man I must obviously be in love with, though I don't feel it now—was I passionate? Did I desire his attention? Or did I merely lie limp and unresisting? Awful, awful questions to ask oneself. Why am I thinking of such? I am the oldest Daughter of the Moon. I may choose my lovers as I wish. Why would I be with a man I didn't want?

"You were good." His words, so soft but heavy still, carry the weight of truth. "You liked it a lot."

These statements . . . I stare back at him. His gaze is fully focused on me. His pupils dilate, and the whites of his eyes gleam. No one else has ever looked at me as he has, as if they saw straight into my soul . . .

I feel it then. I wanted it. I was good. What we shared was good. The lump in my throat dissolves. I am in control of myself again.

He opens his arms, and it is an invitation to an embrace. I crawl up, and rest my head against his chest that rises and falls with his steady breaths. His skin, covered with thick black hair, radiates the warmth I need. He isn't muscular like a soldier, but wiry akin to a man who takes no pleasure in eating. With no sheet to cover me, I am similarly exposed to his scrutiny. It does frighten me to be like this.

"Celestia . . ." He draws another circle on my forehead. This calms me more than any words ever could. "You are very important to me."

And as if he had pushed thick clouds aside, everything becomes so clear to me. What came to pass wasn't an accident, a misjudged moment of lust. I have been drawn to this man, the great Gagargi Prataslav, for almost a year now. He was the first to listen to my concerns when I realized that the empire teeters on the edge of change. He spoke only facts when others beautified them. He agreed that drastic measures might need to be taken. And it was he who . . . Or was it me? It doesn't matter which one of us first mentioned the possibility of a coup.

I snuggle against him, and as I shift, a sticky rivulet coils around the inside of my thigh. I am torn in mind and body alike. This pain is but one of the many prices to be paid. Yet for some reason, I am more ashamed of this than the fact that I am about to depose my own mother.

"There is nothing to feel ashamed of." The gagargi wraps his arms around me. I brush his oiled braid aside and bury my cheek against his chest. How did I bear to harbor such horrid thoughts earlier? He has always been a frugal man, who never gave in to the pleasures that would have been available plenty in the court. He placed the best of our people above himself, something Mother failed to do. "Yours is the empire. Our children will rule it in peace. For that is what you want, isn't it?"

And . . . yes, that is what I want. Peace and prosperity for the Crescent Empire. This great man, Gagargi Prataslav, he wouldn't have tricked me into anything. For he always promised to wait for me, for the day I am ready.

On the eve of the coup, I have to be ready.

We are in his laboratory now, both dressed up; though, without a servant to help me, not all of my gown's buttons are fastened. The long, narrow room has neither a fireplace nor a coal brazier, for he prefers low temperatures when working with souls. The draft finds its way onto my shoulder blades. Lingering in the doorway, I adjust my shawl. Better to hide my state of undress than risk causing rumors or catching cold.

"Do come in. Close the door." Gagargi Prataslav sits at the back of the room, on a three-legged stool before a massive desk littered with soul beads and the instruments of his art. His braided head is bent down in concentration, and he murmurs incantations under his breath. He is holding something white on his lap, and that something is big and alive.

A part of me wants to see where his relentless pursuit of knowledge has led him this time around. Another part of me already knows, and this calls forth shivers that ripple down the whole length of my body. This room is also in the cellar, and dust clings to the row of tiny windows above the desk. My father can't see us here either. I push the door closed behind me and enter the gagargi's den . . . I shake my head sharply, for this drowsiness that ever accompanies me these days has tangled my thoughts once more.

"What are you working on?" I ask. The gagargi should be preparing himself already. We should be preparing ourselves. It is a mere two hours until midnight.

But the gagargi is too absorbed in his incantations to answer. I must go to him to find the answer. And so I do.

The laboratory is lit with soul beads, the harsh white light of ospreys and hawks. Black wrought-iron lanterns hang from the low ceiling and the hooks attached to the un-tapestried brick wall. I pass the small round table where his dinner lays, without doubt untouched, under the silver dome. Next to it is a candelabrum that holds five speckled soul beads. Owls, perhaps. But even in the plenitude of light, this place is haunted by shadows. The animals that enter the room leave it without their souls.

I breathe deep and unclamp my fingers from the folds of my shawl. I need not fear here, with him.

Gagargi Prataslav toured me around the house once, the second or third time I visited him on my own—I can no longer remember the details. He doesn't entertain. He doesn't hold servants. The rooms that aren't occupied by his apprentices are filled with cages of domestic birds and birds of prey alike. Not all of them are white. And not all the animals are birds. In the room that always has a roaring fire he keeps big black apes imported from the south at a great cost. He has been experimenting with them a lot lately, and part of it is from my urging. I think. Our plan for the better empire has but one weakness. The Great Thinking Machine requires human souls for fuel.

"The machine needs the intelligence to calculate the results correctly, just as any other being needs their soul to guide them through their lives." Gagargi Prataslav turns on his stool, replying to my unasked question. As I meet his gaze, I veer to a halt. Though he has never claimed so, I believe he can catch glimpses of the world beyond this one, a skill that has been lost to the empresses for centuries, a secret guarded most closely. "Look at this swan, for example."

I can only break the eye contact upon his prompt. No matter how curious I was earlier to see what he was doing, this couldn't compete with his undivided attention. Now, as he so told me, I look at that big white something: a swan that isn't quite alive anymore, but not yet dead either.

The sacred messenger of my family rests on the gagargi's lap. The bird's webbed feet clutch at his black robes. Its neck is looped around his right arm, and its elegant head rests on his palm. The bird's beady eyes have already glassed over, but its folded wings shift with its faltering breaths.

Why a swan? I want to ask. Why my family's heraldic charge and not some other animal? What spell does he need the bird's soul for? I have seen him separate a soul from the body a hundred times or more. But swans are . . . they are reserved for ceremonies, not for him or anyone else to practice his art. The gagargi smiles, revealing his slightly crooked teeth, and it is almost as if he were amused by my confusion.

"What is there to look at?" I avert my gaze from both him and the swan that is about to die. It annoys me that he is playing guessing games with me. There is precious little time left. Not for me to change my mind, but to prepare ourselves for the coup. Perhaps it would be better if I left now. My carriage has been waiting for me for hours already. "I . . ."

"You should stay," he suggests, and it is as he says. I want to stay with him. In any case, I will be allowed entry to the palace, no matter what time I arrive. Only guards that are sympathetic to the cause man the posts tonight. With my seed, the great General Monzanov, supporting us, there was no difficulty in finding such soldiers. "Observe."

Gagargi Prataslav hums an incantation as he gently strokes the swan's back. The way he focuses on each caress reminds me of Merile and her dogs. My sisters . . . they might hate me after tonight, for having to send mother to Angefort. For a while, there won't be balls or concerts or any of the other frivolities Elise so enjoys. Sibilia might have to settle for a less extravagant debut than the one she has been dreaming of. Merile will be fine as long as she has her dogs. The three of them will adapt, but little Alina, with her mind already so fragile . . .

What will become of her? But this is a risk I must take. Eventually, if the Moon shines bright, they will come to see I was right to take action, that there really was no other choice. The Crescent Empire, such as it is, can't continue to exist. I must depose mother, and eventually marry the Moon.

"Contrary to the popular belief..." The gagargi's voice draws my attention back to him. He twirls his forefinger and middle finger back and forth in a pattern too complex to describe with mere words. The swan twitches. Its black beak parts, revealing a pale pink tongue, but no cry comes out. Instead, the thinnest of white wisps protrudes through its eyes, faint but impossibly strong at the same time. The beak clenches shut, but it is too late. The wisp coils through the air, around the gagargi's fingers like rings spun from mist. "It is possible to extract only a part of a soul."

This I didn't know, and it is an honor to have such information bestowed on me. Curious now, I meet the swan's gaze. Its eyes are dull, but the bird is still very much alive. "What does it mean for the bird?"

The gagargi gets up, rising to his full, towering height, and only a palm's width remains between his head and the ceiling. He unloops the swan's neck from around his arm and then offers the bird to me. "It depends."

I glide the rest of the way to him and hold my hands out, for what else could I do? Yet nothing could have prepared me for the weight of the bird, the stiffness of its body, the oily sheen of its feathers. My knees buckle, but the neck remains looped, just as he left it, with the head perched in a perpetual tilt. How can the bird remain so still?

The gagargi plucks a down feather from the sleeve of his black robes. He raises it to the eye level of the bird, then lets go of it. The feather drifts down, finding the currents of the laboratory's persistent draft. "Done with great skill, by taking the strands of the soul that affect autonomy, the subject becomes unresisting and obedient."

As if suspended by an invisible string, the feather floats just above the floor. Then it touches the cold stone tiles and settles there. The swan remains unmoving in my trembling arms. The gagargi meets my gaze. His eyes bear the strangest sort of fondness, but his mouth is drawn into a . . . smirk?

I can't bear the weight of the swan any longer. I lower it onto the stool, more unceremoniously than it deserves. The bird retains its unnatural position. Will it be frozen in this posture for the rest of its life? If so, I can't imagine a crueler torture. That can't be the purpose of this demonstration. Souls shouldn't be played with. Not even animal ones.

"Can you . . ." The thought is almost too horrifying for me to voice. But we need the Great Thinking Machine to calculate the optimal decisions for us, and the Great Thinking Machine needs a constant supply of its terrible fuel. That is the weak point of our plan, something the gagargi has been working relentlessly to overcome. Is this his solution?

The gagargi grunts, or perhaps chuckles, I am not sure, and I am not sure why it occurs to me to think he might be amused. He lowers his hand on the swan's head once more. His lips move, and he twirls his fingers. A few heartbeats later, a thicker wisp coils through the bird's left eye. He snaps his fingers, and the bird falls limp. The neck can no longer support the weight of the delicate head. The head plunges down and ends up with the parted beak mere inches from the ground. Oblivious to this, the gagargi curls his fingers into a fist around the last wisp. He picks up from his desk an empty—I think—glass sphere no bigger than a child's fist. He hums a short incantation, and as he opens his hand, the wisps are gone, inside the soul bead. But something must have gone wrong. A swan bead should glow white. Instead, this one bears a pale yellow hue.

I in turn study the dead bird and the gagargi. For some reason it feels as if I have had this very same conversation with him before. That I have forgotten it more than once. I feel distanced from myself, almost . . . almost as if I were watching myself from afar. But still I have to ask, "Can you do this to a person?"

The gagargi inspects the soul bead, nodding to himself as if pleased with his handiwork. The white swirls bear a definite yellow hue. I am sure of it. But the question to which I am waiting for an answer is too important for me to get sidetracked by trivialities.

"I can."

The relief is such that I must seek support from the desk. There is no free surface, and pieces of metal and glass press sharp against my palms. I don't care. This breakthrough must be recent. It fills in the last missing piece in our plan. I am grateful, so very grateful, but also drowsy. But tonight is an important night for my empire. I can't allow myself the luxury of feeling tired.

"Yours will be a different empire." The gagargi places the swan bead on the desk, amongst the cogs and wheels and pliers, empty glass spheres and golden springs and pieces of silver cable. The light of the newly created bead meets green and blue. "The time has come to put an end to mindless waste. No more children starving to death. No more soldiers sent to certain death."

His voice is like the sweetest nectar. He places his long

fingers on my right shoulder. His gaze is luminous, lit with promises of the better world. But my attention is drawn to the green and blue that emanates from . . . Alina's name day gift.

"The Great Thinking Machine," I whisper. My youngest sister was almost as afraid of the mechanical peacock as she was of the Great Thinking Machine. I remember promising to take the peacock away, but not bringing it here. How curious that is. How curious of me to think of it now that it is certain that the coup can't fail.

"People will accept our guidance. They are ready for the machine." The gagargi leans toward me in that way of his that I at first found intimidating, then later on irresistible. For he is fully focused on me, and only me. "Adult souls, though tarnished by name and past deeds, will suffice at first. There will be volunteers and those volunteered. Convicted prisoners. War criminals. Engineer Alanov has made extensive calculations and projections. Even if we cannot extract the whole soul at first, partial extraction will suffice for the first year."

His words wash over me, so comforting. I tried my best to comfort Alina. But, haunted as she was by her visions, her grim imagination, there was nothing I could do to make her feel better. But perhaps time will heal her. And what was that last thing the gagargi said to me?

"What happens after the first year?"

He cups my cheeks, lips a mere paper's width apart from me. He is more intoxicating than any wine I have ever tasted. "There will be more volunteers. Once the Great Thinking Machine brings the people equality, or at least the promise of equality, they will not want to go back."

I don't want to go back either, and there is no return anyway to the idealistic, simple childhood of mine where things were ever golden and unchanged. The old world, that of traditions, that of my foremothers, will come to an end soon. The new world, that of machines that can count and equality for all, is upon us.

"Imagine an average family in the countryside, dwelling in one of those villages that are not even marked on the maps. The father works in a dwindling coal mine. The mother takes care of the pitiful cottage. They have six children. The four boys are conscripted to war. Years later, one or none comes back. The father dies of a lung disease. The mother and daughters fall to poverty and starve. It is likely they won't survive the next winter."

This is the reality, what has become of the mighty Crescent Empire. Mother has been so keen on expanding the borders that she has forgotten the price. And though I have tried to make her see that, she has chosen to remain blind. I wonder what would have happened to the empire if it weren't for the gagargi and me, my seed, and the people ready to sacrifice themselves for the cause that is most just.

"These people are never heard of, never seen." The gagargi's mouth is so close to mine that we might as well be kissing. As he exhales, I inhale. I drink the wisdom he shares so willingly. "Imagine they were offered an option. What if there were a tax that applied to everyone, regardless of their birth and origin?"

This is my cue. I have asked this before. I have heard the answer before. But I can't stop myself, not when nothing separates us anymore. "What would we tax?"

The gagargi kisses me. His mouth is hot against mine as he pries my teeth apart with his persistent tongue. Soon, it throbs inside me, though I didn't invite him in. Yet I can't tell him to go away, because I need him. Because I want him.

I think.

He breaks the kiss too soon, and I want to beg him to continue. But before I can do so, he simply says, "Every other child."

I blink, abashed that I got distracted by a kiss, of all things, when we were discussing matters of state. Tax every other child? But of course, he has told me this before. He has kissed me before. I followed him into his bed, under his sheets.

"My studies have confirmed that children's souls are the purest form of energy. Their souls are easily extracted whole. Nothing goes to waste."

It is because I have my gaze averted from his, my head bent down, that I catch a glimpse of the mechanical peacock again. No matter how I always tell Alina that her fears are irrational, she is certain the gagargi means to feed her to the Great Thinking Machine. I think the bird reminded her of that, just as it now reminds me of my sister's disquietude.

But in the light of the gagargi's words, perhaps she is right. No. Nonsense. Why would I think such? Even if some people were willing to gift their soul or their children's souls for the better of the empire, for the Great Thinking Machine, my little sister has nothing to fear. Of that I am almost sure.

"Celestia, tell me, what are you thinking?"

I keep my chin stubbornly pressed down. It is almost a crime itself to doubt him who has placed himself at such great risk on my behalf. After all, if anyone were to find out that we are plotting a coup, if we were to fail tonight, it would be exile for me, execution for him.

"You are filled with such good intentions," I reply, for how could I refuse him? Yet at the same time I ask myself, how does the gagargi know all this that he is sharing with me? Has he been experimenting with people more extensively without keeping me informed? It wouldn't be difficult for him to get a child from an orphanage or a workhouse. It would be easy for his apprentices to dispose of a body.

"Of course I am." He prods my chin up, to meet his eyes. I blink rapidly, a futile attempt to keep my thoughts straight. "Ours will be a merciful empire. But it will only come to be if you play your assigned part."

His gaze locks on to me, and his words bind me. What am I doing resisting him, discarding the sweet bliss of his guidance? I can't afford second thoughts now. I must—

Someone knocks at the door.

———

"Ah, it's time," Gagargi Prataslav says, and pulls his hand away from my chin. His gaze, however, remains locked with mine. He doesn't seem fully satisfied with me. "Do enter."

Captain Janlav steps in. He bears proudly the midnight blue uniform with silver epaulets and crescent buttons, but he wears red gloves. He has a rifle strapped across his back and a curving, ceremonial sword at his hip. He clicks his heels together in a salute and says, "Gagargi Prataslav, everything is ready."

Captain Janlav notices me only then. He offers me a crisp bow and, as he straightens his back, a knowing smile, as if we shared something more than the same side in the coup to come. What could that possibly be?

Then I remember, and again I feel foolish. Elise has lately been sneaking out with him almost every night. My silly sister thinks I don't know, but nothing can escape the gagargi. He has a thousand eyes and a thousand ears. Ours is the just cause. Together, with the people and my seed on our side, we can't lose.

"Good." Gagargi Prataslav glances at me from the corner of his eye. My skin suddenly gets goose bumps. Somehow he knows that I thought ill of him earlier, even if it was only for a fleeting moment. "Stay," he says to me, and strides to the door to confer with the captain.

My stomach knots so tight it hurts. I have displeased him on the eve of the coup, the time I need him the most. Perhaps my mind is in some ways as weak as Alina's. But weakness isn't something an empress-to-be can afford. I pick up the mechanical peacock. I will not let my nerves get the better of me.

"The men are at their assigned places," Captain Janlav reports to Gagargi Prataslav. It is clear the gagargi doesn't want me involved in the conversation. It is my own fault.

I turn the peacock in my hands. There, the spring is under the folded tail of iridescent blue-green feathers. I wind the spring before I set the bird back on the desk. Instantly, it starts pecking at invisible seeds, the magnificent tail balancing the movement.

"When the clock strikes twelve, we wake up the daughters and escort them into the observatory. The curtains are already drawn shut."

I glance at the tiny row of windows above the gagargi's desk. It might be just my imagination, but the Moon seems to shine brighter. Oh, father, you must know that I take no pleasure in the thought of yanking my sisters out of bed, of herding them through the hallways manned by unfamiliar faces. But it is of the utmost importance they don't know about our plan. For if something were to go wrong, it must be only I who face the consequences, not them.

The gagargi asks something in a low voice not meant for my ears. Captain Janlav answers as loudly as before. It is good he doesn't detect the rift between the gagargi and me. "The train is ready, too."

When the peacock's head is next raised, I place my little finger under its path. I wait for the beak to fall and pierce my skin. A heartbeat later it does so. I close my eyes and wince in the pain I deserve. Why did I have to start doubting the gagargi? Have I endangered our plans, the coup?

Once my family is gathered in the sacred observatory, I will explain my terms. Mother will step aside willingly and join her sisters in exile. She will order her bodyguards to surrender. There will be no need to spill the blood of my people. It is an inconvenience that I can't marry the Moon before mother ceases to be, but I am sure my people will accept me as a ruler with Gagargi Prataslav at my side.

"I have handpicked the soldiers for the journey," Captain Janlav continues, eyes wide with boyish enthusiasm, square chin angled up. "Servants we change at every stop on the way to Angefort."

A single drop of blood glistens in the Moon's light. It isn't my imagination. His light really is stronger now. It cascades through the windowpanes as if there were no veil of dust. It brushes the mechanical peacock to a glorious shine. It bends around the swan bead, and the yellow strands turn golden.

I whisper before I can stop myself, "My father is listening to us."

Gagargi Prataslav's head snaps in my direction. For a moment, his jaw hangs slack. Then he pulls his hood up and says, "Step away from the light, Celestia."

His is the voice I have listened to and obeyed without hesitation. Until tonight, at least. But as I bask in the Moon's light, I don't understand why I, the empress-to-be, have done so. My little finger still bleeds. On the desk, the mechanical peacock continues swinging back and forth. Peck, peck, peck goes its golden beak against the scarred surface.

"Join us here." The gagargi motions at Captain Janlav. The soldier glances at the gagargi, at me. He doesn't understand what is happening either. "The time has come for you to take your mother's place and lead this empire into the age of progress."

"The age of progress," I repeat before I can stop myself. It is as if he has wound some invisible spring inside me. As if he could control me even from across the room, long after winding up the spring.

Behind me, the peacock continues pecking.

"The age of unity." Captain Janlav's eyes shine with fervor. Is he equally affected by the gagargi's manipulation? How many others does the gagargi have under his influence? By what means did he achieve this?

Though I yearn to drift to the gagargi, I force myself to remain in the Moon's light. Next to me, the swan lies limp on the stool, dead. Its soul swirls inside the glass bead, the golden strands strengthening more with each heartbeat. I pick the bead up to examine it closer. For there is something about it that—

"Celestia?" The way the gagargi says my name stings like a needle. "Put it down, dear. I have told you before not to tamper with my experiments."

A chastisement? Since when has anyone apart from mother had the right to chastise me? I hold on to the soul bead with both my hands, and yet a part of me wants to set it back on the desk. It shouldn't be difficult for me to do as I wish. But it is, and I have to say something. "I will not drop it."

"No, you won't." Gagargi Prataslav looms at me from the door, clearly barely able to resist the urge to stride to me. I realize he doesn't want to step into the Moon's light. He is afraid of my father. As he should be.

"Captain Janlav," I say, bolder now. I no longer know how the night will play out, and even if I could, I wouldn't try to stop the coup. The Crescent Empire can't continue to exist as it is. And yet, I have to find out if there is something the gagargi isn't telling me.

Captain Janlav blinks, and with that he is more present again. He stares keenly at me, for it is an honor to be addressed by a Daughter of the Moon. I say, "On a night like this, many things might go wrong. I trust you will personally take care of my sisters' safety."

"The train is ready . . ." He glances sideways at the gagargi, frowning. He clenches his mouth shut. He folds his arms behind his back.

"The train is ready for my mother," I say, even as the gagargi glares daggers at me. I cradle the bead in my open palms. The glass feels warm against my skin. "That is what you mean, is it not?"

"Be still." Gagargi Prataslav lifts his right forefinger up before Captain Janlav can reply. The soldier's eyes go blank. Indeed, the gagargi has the soldier under his power. "Listen only to me."

Then the gagargi turns his full attention to me, and when he speaks his voice is thick with what could be concern, but is actually . . . a suggestion. "Celestia, are you feeling unwell?"

If I were so inclined, if I were to want to return to the sweet bliss of ignorance, I would only have to say yes.

"We have gone through this countless times before. Do you not remember?"

It is as if he is giving me the permission to remember, and then I do remember everything so clearly that I can't fathom how I could ever have forgotten it. The train is for my sisters. It is better for them to be sent away, in case unrests follow the coup. But what about mother, then? What did the gagargi say about her?

"A deposed empress would pose a risk to our rule." The words form on my lips on their own, and it isn't me who is talking but someone else altogether.

The gagargi nods in paternal approval. "And what must we do with anything that places our plans at risk?"

"We . . ." *must eliminate all risks.*

"Yes?"

"She . . ." *must die for me to marry the Moon.*

I realize these are his words, not mine. I will not say them. Not now. Not ever. Even if I may have condemned my mother before, now that I have regained my senses, I will not order her executed.

The gagargi's thin lips draw back, revealing his crooked teeth. "Out with it."

But my father's light is pure silver. The bead in my cupped palms blooms in amber. It is the key to everything. The Great Thinking Machine needs human souls for fuel. A human soul is amber in color. I think of the swan, how the gagargi stroked its forehead. I think of myself, lying with my head on his lap as he drew circles on my forehead and muttered words of . . . devotion, I assumed, but what if . . .

No, it is too terrible, too horrifying to even think of. I have wanted this empire to change for as long as I can remember. Gagargi Prataslav and I share the same goals. He would never . . . I glance at him, and find him staring hungrily at me from the other side of the room.

Oh, he would. He would have me order my mother executed, have me marry the Moon without ever realizing what I was doing. For even as my father can see into my soul, if I were still under the gagargi's spell, I would think it my idea and my father wouldn't turn me aside.

"I will not do it." I lift the bead higher, before my face, and bask in the glow that is both disquieting and comforting. My hands tremble with my fury. But my voice is as regal as ever. "Even if you have somehow managed to steal a part of my soul."

"Don't you dare to—" The gagargi strides toward me then, regardless of the Moon's light. His black robes flap in his wake. His boots strike hard against the rough stone floor.

"Stop." I extend my hands toward the gagargi. The bead rolls so close to the edge of my fingertips that I am sure it will fall. Yet, somehow, it remains there, but only barely.

The gagargi halts as if he has hit a wall. He offers his palms at me in a pacifying gesture. But as he speaks, his nostrils flare. They are red inside, as if he were about to bleed. "Everything is all right. Nothing has changed. Just put the bead down, Celestia. Let us talk in peace."

This is the confirmation I needed. If I put the bead down, he will regain his control over me, I am sure of that. And after my defiance, he will extract even more of my soul, until nothing remains but an automaton crafted for his purposes. It is awful to realize the truth. I really don't matter to him—a soulless shell would suffice. For with me by his side, married to the Moon and bearing his child, he could rule the empire all by himself.

"Everything has changed." I pry my palms apart. The bead rolls into the widening gap, so bright now. I have lost a part of myself irrevocably. But I would rather lose it permanently than let a man like Gagargi Prataslav possess control over me. "I will not become one of your soulless automatons."

The Moon blesses me with his strength. I part my hands. For a moment, the bead just floats there, suspended in the air. Then it drops. Slowly, slower than it should. The gagargi dashes toward me, regardless of what my father might see. But it is too late.

The bead shatters as it meets the floor. The impact jars my every bone and muscle, as if I were the one slammed against the cold tiles. I fold onto my knees, spreading my arms to brace for the impact.

Golden haze blinds me. Pain binds me. It is my enemy that I have to thank for recovering from this daze.

"You stupid, stupid girl," the gagargi shrieks, descending to all fours before me. He lifts one hand up, fingers twirling shapes. I realize he is trying to capture the soul strands that coil above the shattered bead.

He may not have them. But how does one capture back one's soul? The strands coil toward me like a lost child rushing to greet her mother. Could it be as simple as to . . .

I bend my head down and inhale as deep as my lungs allow, even more, until it feels like they will explode. The shimmering tastes familiar, of midsummer roses in bloom mixed with endless fields of pristine snow. Even upon the first breath, I feel invigorated, stronger, faster. I inhale more, and I see . . . green grass under bare feet. Mist rolling to cover poppy fields. Alina laughing as she runs through dawn. Merile petting her dogs in a white wicker chair. Sibilia dreaming of her debut, of short-sleeved, sequined dresses. Elise sparkling on the dance floor, red-gold curls forming a halo around her head. But I can also see and smell and taste and feel the blue skies that stretch on forever and clear-watered blue lakes that are perfect for nesting.

"Stop resisting me," the gagargi curses, and slaps my cheek. The impact is so hard that my head lolls sideways. The memories fade with the sudden, blooming pain. But they aren't lost. If I were to want to do so, I could easily recall them.

"Never," I hiss, even as sparks cling to the edges of my vision. Defiantly, I fan the air between us, bringing the last lingering amber strands toward me. I suck in the air. This is my soul, not his to toy around with.

Gagargi Prataslav, still on all fours like a snarling bear, raises a paw at me. He attempts to push at my shoulder, but I evade him gracefully. He growls at me, "What is mine will be mine forever."

But that is where he is wrong. He may have fooled me once, but he will never fool me again. There are no soul strands left for him to catch. "You will never have me."

I feel whole again, or at least in control of myself. Whatever I have lost, I can hopefully regain with time. I get back up on my knees. I sway onto my feet. I need to make it out of here, back to the palace to warn my family.

"Celestia, Celestia . . ." The gagargi stares at me from under his thick, black brows, and then he rises to his full height. He is tall, dark, and menacing. How I ever found him anything else, I don't know. I regret that mistake, even as I know that will not be enough. Unless . . .

Captain Janlav stands by the door, staring fixedly ahead. He truly is under the gagargi's control. If I can dash past the gagargi, I might make it past him, too.

"My little defiant empress-to-be." The gagargi's gaze deepens, widens. I can feel his voice winding around me. He can't resist trying to see if he can still manipulate me. I steel my mind against him. I brush his words aside.

"Ah!" The gagargi taps his forehead theatrically. But this experiment of his, it has revealed that I can stand up against him now. "Ah, my dearest Celestia, it is of no use to fight against me. When the revolution comes we must all choose whether we are with the victors or whether we are but one of the victims."

"Without me by your side," I say, spitting the words out, circling around him, forcing myself to maintain the eye contact, until it is me who is closer to the door, "you will never rule the empire."

Mother will believe me. My seed will believe me. Together, we can craft a plan. Surely we can prevent this coup attempt from turning into the revolution the gagargi desires.

"Well . . ." The gagargi stares at me, and his dark gaze intensifies. In it lies a challenge. And more. I recognize treachery now. "We shall just have to see how things pan out tonight, won't we?"

I flee to the door then, past the dazed Captain Janlav, out of the laboratory. I don't dare to look back as I scamper up the steep stairs, away from the gagargi's ghastly chambers, into the entrance hall. I must stop what I have started. I must protect my mother and sisters.

"Run, my dearest Celestia, run!" Gagargi Prataslav's words roll against my back, cold and heavy like waves about to drag one under the surface. "You may run as fast as your little feet can carry, but you will be too late. The revolution starts tonight, and you will be safe only with me!"

I push the hall's double doors open with both hands and sway into the freezing, black night. Even though my carriage is waiting for me, I fear the gagargi may be right. Everything is ready for the coup. By the time I reach the palace, it will be too late to stop it. There will be blood, and some of it may be my family's.

I glance up at the sky, at the Moon's glowing face. Oh, Father, please help your strayed daughter!

Chapter 6

Alina

As soon as Nurse Nookes closes the door behind her, I open my eyes, as I have done on every single night since my name day. I will stay awake for as long as I can and longer. At some point, I might fall asleep. Though I've asked my sisters and even Nurse Nookes how to distinguish dreams from reality, I'm still unsure of what happens in my room after the lights go out, and I don't dare to ask more questions, lest they start worrying even more about me.

Shadows live in the world beyond this one. As I'm the youngest, it's impossible for me to see there. And yet, the shadows arrive mere moments later.

I lie very quiet under my down-feather duvet as they shift in the corners of the room, as their forms strengthen. The shadows are smaller here than in life. Diminished. I can't yet name who has come to visit me tonight. Usually it's birds, but sometimes animals I've never met in life.

Tonight I'm visited by a swan, an owl, and a hairy creature that stoops on two legs. It's a monkey. No, it's bigger. An ape. I nod a greeting to the animals, but I don't dare to speak, lest someone may hear me and alert Nurse Nookes. I can still taste the sugary mixture she urged me to swallow before tugging me to bed. I spat it out when she had her back turned to me. I know she means well, everyone does, but I hate how her potions cloud my mind.

As always, my animal visitors play out scenes from their lives. Their shadows dance dark against the white wall opposite my bed. I watch each of their performances, stifling yawns, forcing my eyes to stay open.

The swan flies, flies to faraway lands, to nest and raise its hatchlings on the shores of a clear-watered lake.

The owl hunts. It swoops over glittering snowfields, toward the sounds it hears from under the snow banks. Then it dives, talons spread. Its beak pierces the ice-crusted snow. The scene ends in the owl's victory. In a mouse's death.

The ape leads a slow life. It clings to a tree and munches leaves of plants I don't recognize. It scratches its friends, and they scratch it in return.

Though I can't know for sure, I think these might be the best moments of the animals' lives. It's well possible that some of my visitors have shown me what they wished they'd done differently. In any case, be it memories or regrets, it's my duty to watch, since if I don't watch then I fear that no one else will do so.

After the ape retreats back into the corner, I nod again at the shadows. They nod back at me. It's so hard not to yawn, to remain awake. Sometimes each animal has only one scene to play. Sometimes several. Sometimes they share with me what might be their nightmares. I don't know for sure.

The shadows slip onto the wall together. Each performs the same story. They're caught and caged. They're taken to a house I don't want to name for fear of somehow summoning *his* attention. Their cages are carried down a steep staircase, into a long, narrow room and . . . after that the animals cease to be as they were and only their shadows remain as their own.

"How can I help you?" I whisper as loudly as I dare. I've

asked this before. They never reply, just stare back at me. Maybe I'm the only one willing to hear of their fates. To remember rather than to ignore and forget.

The swan stirs from its posture of defeat. It unfolds its wings from against its sides and raises its head high. The beak parts, and . . .

"Alina?"

I scramble back on my bed. The swan spoke to me. It knows my name.

The owl and ape stare at me. They seem as confused as I feel.

"Alina?" the voice asks again. It doesn't belong to the swan but to Nurse Nookes.

"Hide," I whisper to the animals.

The swan tilts its head. The owl looks as if it were about to hoot. The ape merely scratches its armpit.

"I'm coming in," Nurse Nookes calls through the door, even though she received no reply.

"Hide!" I command the stubborn animals, even as I slip farther under my fluffy duvet and pat it smooth around me.

But only as the door creaks open, the shadows scatter back into the corners. Relief eases the knot in my stomach. If you don't know where to look, you won't see them. I learned of their presence only after I got my name.

"It's me . . ." Nurse Nookes slips into my room, shading a duck-soul lantern. Her low heels tap softly against the carpet though she's round like the plumpest of summer apples. I think she could move silently if she so wanted, but she makes sounds so as not to frighten me in case I'd stir to her entrance. "Nurse Nookes."

I quickly close my eyes before she notices I never went to sleep in the first place. What is she doing in my room when I've done nothing to warrant anyone's attention? I haven't cried or shouted in my sleep, I'm sure of it! And it can't be morning yet. I've stayed awake through so many nights that I know the hours that lie between this moment and the relief that dawn brings in its wake.

Maybe I did fall asleep. This might be a dream. It's also well possible this is a nightmare. If it is, I hope that it won't be one of those where the gagargi threatens to feed me to his Great Thinking Machine.

"You must wake up." Nurse Nookes shakes my shoulder, voice shaded by worry, of all things. But something is off. I've known her since I was born, and tonight her concern has nothing to do with me.

Be this a dream or a nightmare, I can't leave her facing it alone. She's always been there for me, even if it's been with her potions. I turn to my side, to face her, and rub my eyes as if she'd woken me up. "What is it?"

Nurse Nookes peels the duvet off me. She doesn't look at me when she speaks. "The Crescent Empress has summoned you and your sisters to the sacred observatory."

This is . . . This might still be a dream. It certainly doesn't feel like reality. Nurse Nookes is never afraid of anything. Mama has never summoned me or my sisters to the sacred observatory in the middle of the night. Dreams, on the other hand, are full of people acting out of order, and other pure impossibilities. Running, but never reaching your destination. Packing, but never remembering everything. Those sort of things.

I hide a small smile. When you realize you're in a dream, sometimes it's possible to control it. I crawl to sit on the bed and dangle my legs over the edge.

Nurse Nookes squats down before me, as she always does. She looks me squarely in the eye, frowns like drapes drawn apart. "Do you need to use the pot-pot?"

I shake my head, though rather to hide my secrets from her than in reply. In any case, I don't feel like I'd need to pee anytime soon. Either not enough hours have passed since she tugged me into bed or this is indeed a dream.

"Can you take off the nightgown while I fetch your clothes?"

My insides squirm as the wrongness sharpens. A Daughter of the Moon never dresses or undresses by herself. Of course I shouldn't keep Mama waiting. But this need for haste . . . Nurse Nookes wouldn't ask this of me unless we're in a great hurry.

I tug the nightgown over my head while Nurse Nookes rummages in the clothes room.

"Something warm. Something . . ." she mutters in the dark. Why she hasn't switched on the lights, I can't guess. "Can't waste more time. This will have to do."

I jump down from the bed as she waddles to me. She clutches a thick winter dress against her very round bosom. It's not the kind of dress I'd usually wear for an audience with Mama. But rather . . .

"Are we going somewhere?" In my ears, the question rings like a squeal.

"Perhaps" is all that Nurse Nookes replies.

Nurse Nookes rushes through the buttons. Then she orders me to sit down, and quickly pulls fur-lined boots on my feet. She squats down before me again. I look past her, at the shadows hiding in the corners.

"There, there." She gently pinches my cheeks. Her voice is cheery, but I don't think she feels that way. "I believe you are ready."

Before I can reply, a knock comes from the door. There is nothing cheery or timid about this one. Rather, it sounds . . .

furious. I know it then for sure. This is a nightmare.

"We're coming!" Nurse Nookes shouts, but it seems to me she'd prefer to curse. She strides to the door and waves at me to follow.

The shadows hover hesitantly in the corners. They want to come with me. I don't know what to do.

Nurse Nookes is about to open the door just as whatever horrendous creature waiting behind it knocks again, louder. At the moment that she's not looking at me, I lift my hem and beckon to the shadows. "Quick, now."

"Yes, quick." Nurse Nookes pulls the door open.

The shadows dash to hide in my hem. They settle against the wool in an eyeblink, becoming mere darker patches. After all, shadows don't have bodies.

I rush out from my chambers and step into the nightmare.

Six soldiers in midnight blue guard both ends of the hallway. I don't recognize any of the men, whose faces are hard as if chiseled with an ax and whose gazes dart from door to door as if they were expecting trouble. They clutch at the straps of their rifles or the pommels of their viciously curving swords. Curiously, their gloves are red.

As I rub my eyes, a bearded guard strides the length of the corridor. He's the furious knocker, and there is no mercy in his knuckles as he pounds in turn on the doors of Merile, Sibilia, and Elise. He stops by Elise's door, doesn't continue to knock on Celestia's. Why?

One by one, my sisters emerge from their rooms, but not one of them bears the same expression.

Elise waltzes to the hallway in a gleaming white ball gown that glitters with sequins and pearls. Her smile is the widest

I've ever seen, and as she dances toward me she's akin to a dove released from its cage.

Sibilia pushes her head through the door crack. Her red-gold hair, though braided, sticks out in all directions, and her cheeks glow. "What under the Moon is happening here?"

Elise pulls the door open and grabs Sibilia by the elbow. "It's the time, at last. Come!"

Sibilia stumbles after her, a silver hand mirror in her free hand. She's still in her nightgown. Her feet are bare.

None of this makes sense. If this isn't a nightmare, then nothing is. I pinch my arm before Nurse Nookes can stop me. It doesn't help, and Nurse Nookes doesn't notice me trying again either. Two of the soldiers have formed a barrier behind Elise and Sibilia. There is no turning back, no returning to our rooms.

Merile's door swings open last. Her beautiful dogs burst out, unclothed still. My sister dashes after them in her gorgeous fur-trimmed cloak, a dog coat in each hand. "Rafa, Mufu, stop! My darling dears, you'll catch a cold!"

"Rafa . . ." I kneel before I remember the shadows hiding in my hem. As I embrace Rafa, the shadows shy away from her. Mufu bounces to lick my face. "Oh, Mufu!"

Then Merile is there, tugging the coats over their heads and fastening them under their bellies. Rafa and Mufu must have smelled the shadows at last, for they sniff at my hem and their thin tails wag wildly.

"Let's get going, then," the bearded soldier grunts. I glare at him. Who does he think he is to order a Daughter of the Moon!

I'm not the only one who is shocked. Sibilia's face flushes with fury. She brandishes the mirror at the soldier. "In my nightgown?"

But Elise flings an arm around Sibilia. She whispers something I can't quite hear in her ear. All color drains from Sibilia's face. She says, "But of course. We shouldn't keep Mama waiting."

The guards lead us through the silent palace. Down the stairs to the second floor. Through corridors lit by duck-soul lanterns. Past curtained windows. I tremble, want to turn back, want to wake up. But Nurse Nookes ushers me onward.

We make it halfway to the sacred observatory without a word said. If you don't count Rafa's and Mufu's occasional barking and Nurse Nookes's heavy breathing. This silence weighs my steps like a wet cloak with its hood pulled up. I want to toss it aside.

"Sibs . . ." I tug at the sleeve of my sister's nightgown. "Why do you have a mirror with you?"

Elise giggles, the only one of us who's merry. "Yes, do tell us why?"

Color rises to Sibilia's cheeks in tides of red. "I was practicing . . . No, what do you think? I woke up to this wretched knocking, and it was the first thing I found in the dark."

"Be quiet," the guard striding behind us orders. His breath smells of raw onions.

Sibilia glares daggers at him, irritated. "Why?"

The guard runs his fingers down the strap of his rifle. "For your own safety."

Nurse Nookes hastens to my side to shield me from the guard, and seeing her afraid makes me even more so.

We walk the rest of the way in utter, frozen silence. Even Rafa and Mufu refrain from yapping.

The guards halt as we come to the white crescent stairs leading to the sacred observatory. Elise strides up the stairs without hesitation, dragging Sibilia with her. Merile limps after them with her dogs. But I hesitate to follow.

"Nookes . . ." I tug at her arm, so strong and familiar amidst all the strangeness. This doesn't feel like a dream anymore, not even like a nightmare. Everything feels too real. "Nurse Nookes, I'm afraid."

Elise draws to a halt, and so do my other sisters. They stare at me. Are they embarrassed of me, or just worried?

"Don't be," Nurse Nookes replies. "I'll come with you."

But the bearded guard that smells of raw onions places a heavy hand on her round shoulder. He, too, wears a glove as red as if it were dipped in blood. "Only the daughters may enter. That is the order we follow."

I burst into tears then. "I want to wake up! I want to wake up now!"

"Oh dear . . ." Nurse Nookes glares at the bearded guard. The rest of the soldiers have formed a chain around us. The only way out is up the stairs. This can't have escaped Nurse Nookes, but she doesn't seem to care about that. She embraces me with both wobbly arms. "Little Alina, listen to me: sometimes in life you must be very brave. And tonight is one of those nights. You are a Daughter of the Moon. You are blessed by his wisdom and strength. As long as you remember that, nothing in this world can harm you."

But it sounds to me as if she's the one swallowing tears. And suddenly I don't want to be comforted by her, but to comfort her! Her heart knows only kindness. But, I fear, after tonight, it will be full of sorrow.

"Nothing can harm me," I whisper in Nurse Nookes's ear. My skirts shift, I feel it. One of the shadow animals, the owl, is moving. It slips out from under my hem, against Nurse Nookes. I know, just know, that it will look after my . . . my friend. "Nothing can harm you."

A clack of boots against marble comes from the direction of the stairs. I let go of Nurse Nookes just in time to see a soldier I at last recognize by name. Captain Janlav halts on the second-to-last step and lashes a question at the guards. "What is the meaning of this delay?"

The guards all stare at me. I'm an excuse for them. I . . . I will not be afraid. I wipe the tears from my eyes. I won't cry more. No matter what.

I hurry up the stairs, past the soldier to my sister, without as much as glancing over my shoulder. I can feel Nurse Nookes watching me, her gentle heart swelling with sadness and pride.

White silk folds like snow banks against the windows that reach to the ceiling. I stumble on my own feet when I realize that every single curtain of the celestial observatory has been torn down. The Moon fills the vast crescent room with pure, silvery light. My father is blessing us with his presence. He's watching and seeing, listening and hearing.

"My daughters," Mama greets us. She glitters and shines at the very center of the room, on the circular stage under the round glass dome. In her eyes live the ocean and skies, for she's the empire. Celestia waits next to her, as white as our mother, but her right cheek is burning red.

"Come here," Mama summons me and my sisters.

Somehow I know, just know this moment is immeasurably valuable, something to cherish rather than to rush over. My sisters realize this, too. We shuffle slowly and solemnly into an arc before her. The guards remain back even then, at the top of the staircase. That is the only shadowy place left, the only way in and out of the room that has windows for walls.

"Mama." Elise curtsies deep and remains with her sequined

skirts spread wide, head bent down. Her red-gold hair glows under our father's gaze. He loves us dearly.

Mama glides to her and kisses her forehead. She loves us too. "My beautiful Elise."

Sibilia curtsies next, not as effortlessly as Elise, but the Moon winds around her nevertheless. She blushes when she receives her kiss and praise. Then it's Merile's turn.

We rarely receive this much attention from Mama, but when she approaches me, I tremble. This isn't a dream. There's no waking up. The Moon's light blooms around me. The shadows still hide in my hem. He will do what is in his power. I'll do what's in mine.

"My little Alina," Mama whispers as she seals her lips against my temple.

I feel the warmth of her breath, the waver in her voice. And I also feel . . . the swan detaching from my hem. I hold my breath as it folds against Mama's white dress. She doesn't notice a thing, even though she's the empress and thus she should see into the world beyond this one.

I rise from the curtsy, feeling better now that I know the swan's shadows will look after Mama. A thought comes to me, and it comforts me. Maybe it was the Moon who sent the animals to me, to us. If that is so, whom will the ape look after, or will it stay with me?

"My daughters," Mama addresses us again, having climbed up to the circular stage, to Celestia. I realize it then. There was no kiss for my oldest sister. Why? "I have grave news for you. The unrests that have plagued my empire have spread here, to the streets and plazas of the Summer City."

"Are we in danger?" Merile squeals, swooping Rafa up. She tries desperately to also pick up Mufu, but her arms are nowhere near long enough. Mufu, having sensed her mistress's distress, dives to hide under the heavy hem of her cloak.

"Of course we aren't," Elise replies, craning over her shoulder at the soldiers lingering at the top of the stairs. It's almost as if she's expecting Captain Janlav to acknowledge her words, for there is no way for him or any of the other guards to not have heard our conversation. And yet, he stares right past her, as if he'd never seen her in his life.

"How can you be so sure?" Sibilia cries out. She brushes her nightgown's hem. Then slaps Elise's arm with the hand mirror. "To be lured from my bed in the middle of the night! To be ushered through the palace in my nightgown! The shame alone will kill me for sure!"

The faintest of smiles plays on Mama's lips. Elise opens her mouth as if to protest, but clenches it shut at the last possible moment.

"My daughters, I need you to listen to me very, very carefully. It is no longer safe in the Summer City. The guards here will take you via tunnels to the train station. There you will board an imperial train that will take you to a safe place. You shall wait until the unrests have been . . . dealt with. Do you understand this?"

I cling to my braveness, though coldness spreads through my body. Soon my fingers and toes and arms and legs all shake. I fold my arms across my chest. I can't stop the tears.

"Oh, Alina!" Celestia covers her parted lips with her hand. Then she rushes down the stage to me, graceful akin to a swan diving. Her cheek, however she hurt it, glows red, and it must pain her to speak. And yet she says to me, "Here, please take my shawl."

She's too kind. I'm only too afraid. I tremble horribly as she wraps her shawl around my shoulders. She hugs me before heading back. But when she turns around, I notice three things that are so very wrong.

Two buttons midway up her back are unfastened.

She returns to Mama rather than taking her customary place to the right of Elise.

But most worryingly, her shadow is faint, much fainter than those of my other sisters, or even Mama's.

"Celestia." Mama addresses my sister only when she's again next to her. There's a tightness in her voice. Tiredness too. Maybe even a trace of disappointment. But that must be just my imagination, for Celestia has always been Mama's favorite.

Celestia bends her head down as if she'd done something bad. "Yes, Mama."

"I entrust your sisters into your care," Mama says. There's no blame in her voice. How could there be? What could Celestia ever do to deserve such? But what Mama says next resembles a plea terribly, terribly much. "Guard them from any possible harm, regardless of the cost."

Celestia lifts her head up high, and addresses us with confidence that warms me more than her shawl. "I will. This I solemnly swear under the Moon, who shines as my witness."

Mama closes her eyes and exhales deeply. Then a rattle of boots comes from behind us, from the stairs. Mama's eyes fling open. Her forehead creases with a frown, as does Celestia's. My sisters and I spin around just in time to see the guards parting to let a man pass.

And not just any man, but the most terrible and dangerous one of them all.

"Celestia." Gagargi Prataslav halts on the highest step, at the edge of the shadows, as if he belongs with them. He takes in the pulled-down curtains, us basking in the Moon's light. He doesn't seem that interested in Mama or Elise, Sibilia or Merile. But there is still something disturbingly hungry in the way he studies Celestia . . . and me. "Crescent Empress."

"Gagargi Prataslav," Celestia replies, boldly meeting his gaze. It's as if she and he had been opponents in a game, and against all odds my sister had emerged victorious. This is how the scene seems to me. "The winter equinox is here."

The gagargi laughs a throaty chuckle as if Celestia had told a joke. Her pose tenses, and she cranes her neck, her chin up. Maybe I don't know what they're really talking about. Sometimes adults talk of two or more things at once. But this much is clear to me: even if Celestia and Gagargi Prataslav have been playing together, they aren't friends anymore. How this came to pass, I don't know, and I'm not sure I want to find out.

"That it is." Gagargi Prataslav's words form a grim lullaby that summons me to dark currents. I can see them winding around everyone present. It's the same spell he's cast so many times before. The soldiers stiffen as if turning into stone. Elise, Sibilia, and Merile fall still, too. Only Mama, Celestia, and I remain unaffected.

But I pretend stillness. For I know he meant the spell to touch me as well.

Celestia—I can see she must force herself to do so—steps down from the stage and strolls to the gagargi. Her white hem sways in rhythm with her steps, and she shines radiantly under the light of our blessed father. This must give her the strength she so dearly needs, for when she speaks, her voice bears no hint of fear or anger. "Thank you for coming, though it is past midnight."

Mama nods at the words. The veins on her neck stick out, as if drawn with a blue pencil. "Celestia will see the daughters to the train and into safety."

It's a practiced conversation, I realize. Mama and Celestia know more about the unrests than they've shared with me and my sisters. The gagargi, on the other hand . . . he plays some part in all this. I just don't know what part that might be. I don't even know if he's on our side. What a frightening thought . . .

"Is that so?" The gagargi's question only confirms my doubts. His words stick to my ears like honey. I distrust everything sweet for a reason. It's not the gagargi's right to challenge Mama's decisions. He's only an advisor.

"For their own safety." Mama gazes up at the dome and the sky beyond. Can she see what the future holds in store for us? Or is she holding our father accountable for our fates? Mama nods to herself, then faces the gagargi with a faraway gaze that bears the light of the stars. "Celestia, and my younger daughters, are the future of the empire. If any harm were to fall on them, this would endanger what little hope of stability we have for the years to come."

Mama is bargaining. Things aren't going as she planned. But they aren't going as the gagargi planned either. He's in control of the soldiers, but he didn't want them to witness this conversation. This conversation is dangerous to him as well.

Gagargi Prataslav runs his fingers along his shaggy beard as if he really did have the right to consider a command. His bony knuckles crack. The sound echoes in the observatory for a too-long time.

"I will remain here and face the anger of my people," Mama says, folding her arms across her chest. Her back is very straight. Her voice is very even. "People need to know there is a future for them, even if they rebel."

"Besides," Celestia remarks, standing on the edge of the

shadows, so close to the gagargi that I wouldn't dare to do so. The Moon's light forms a bright ring around her. She's terribly white and terribly pale, and her cheek is very red. "There is nothing to be done tonight. My father knows."

I can only barely hold still. Something bad, worse than unrests, has happened. Something between the gagargi and my sister. I'm not sure I want to find out what that might be. I fear that eventually I will.

"I gathered as much." Gagargi Prataslav grunts, a sound of acknowledgment rather than disappointment. He gazes first at Celestia, who stands right before him, then past her at Mama. "Then so be it."

With that, the spell lifts. Beside me Merile gasps, drawing in a long breath that spooks both Rafa and Mufu. Sibilia blinks as though she'd just woken up from a nightmare. Elise flutters her long lashes and rubs her forehead. I realize I should do something, too. I yawn.

"Go." From the gagargi's thin lips, the word is like a whiplash. His tight smile bears a hint of cruel amusement, and I know, just know, that that smile is targeted at me. It says: *Run, run if you want to, but you can never flee from me.*

A tremble runs through my body. I can't, won't turn away from him. He's not the kind of man you let stand behind your back.

"Go now then." The gagargi steps aside, and as he motions at the stairs his voluminous black sleeve spreads like a bat's wing. "But I will send for you when the time is right."

Elise, Sibilia, and Merile are still too confused to understand that though the gagargi seemingly addresses us all, the words are meant for Celestia.

"And I will return," Celestia replies, unswayed by threats, by anything. "Once my sisters are safe."

"Elise, Sibilia, Merile, Alina," Mama calls to us. She has made a deal of some sort. What did it cost her and Celestia? The price must be terrible beyond naming. "It is settled. You must go now."

As my sisters are just stirring from the spell, it takes a moment for them to understand that we are to leave the observatory, the Summer Palace, the whole city. Elise looks excited, Sibilia flushed as she fidgets with her nightgown's sleeves, while Merile merely picks up Rafa and Mufu in turns, unable to decide which one to carry.

"Mama . . ." Celestia calls softly over her shoulder as she prepares to leave. It's a good-bye of sorts. Or that's what I think, at least.

Mama stares at Celestia, her expression impossible to interpret. She glances at the gagargi, at Celestia. Celestia bites her upper lip.

"Wait," Mama orders, though we can't have much time to lose. The gagargi might change his mind and prevent us from leaving. That I fear. And yet, this too is an important moment.

Celestia falls to a deep curtsy as Mama glides to her, faster than is her natural pace. My oldest sister presses her head down, as if she were apologizing. Mama kisses her on the forehead. It's a seal of forgiveness. There is no doubt about that. "Go now in peace, my daughter."

Celestia meets Mama's gaze, their eyes the same blue, behind them the same wisdom. "I will. Thank you, Mama."

My sisters and I leave then, in a single line, in the order of age, as is our habit. As I hurry past the gagargi, I feel my hem shift one last time. The ape detaches from the fabric and slips into the gagargi's robes. He doesn't notice a thing.

I suddenly realize he can't see the shadows.

Chapter 7

Merile

The stink. The day carriage stinks of sweat and the humid air of a train rushing across the empire. I can't escape it, not even when I kiss Mufu's black forehead, still wet from the melting snowflakes. I can't escape anything here, no matter how I try.

"Merile . . ." Alina yawns on the sofa opposite to me. At last. It's afternoon already, but she hasn't slept a wink. Not after the plain breakfast, not when the train stopped for water and coal, not while the nameless servant took Rafa and Mufu for a quick walk outside, not even after the train rattled back into movement.

"Yes?" I pick the dried hare leg from the lacquered side table and hold it out for Mufu to gnaw. Wrong. So many things are so utterly wrong and unacceptable here, but I must try my best to feign that everything is well for little Alina's sake. "What is it?"

Alina pauses brushing Rafa as she glances at Celestia and Elise. They sit on the other end of the carriage, on the padded chairs by the oval table, and pretend to do embroidery. But it wouldn't do to let little Alina know that all is not how it seems, no matter how dearly I want to know myself what really is going on. Eight days. Ever since we boarded this train, eight long days ago, Celestia and Elise have had whispered conversations when they think Alina and I can't hear them. I'm sure they keep Sibilia in the dark, too.

"We're fleeing," Alina whispers, thin fingers clutching the hairbrush's handle so tight her knuckles threaten to pop right through her pale skin. "Aren't we?"

"Huh," I mutter under my breath. Fair. It's not fair she should ask me that question when I don't know the answer. I can only make what Elise would call educated guesses.

This all has something to do with Gagargi Prataslav, the horrid man who threatened my dear companions, and his awful Thinking Machine. Something very bad happened to Celestia, and Elise is upset because of that, or for some completely unrelated reason. Neither of them will speak of it. What they speak of is the unrest amongst the peasants and . . .

"The train is taking us to a safe place." I repeat the lie told to me. Or a partial lie. Both Celestia and Elise agree that we couldn't have stayed in the Summer City. The windows in this train, or at least in the two carriages where we are allowed access, are bolted shut, but I've glimpsed burning buildings through the cracks between the heavy white curtains. At times, the train has sped through cities, only to halt later in smaller towns. The unrests are real and dangerous, whatever they are about.

Alina lowers the brush on the sofa and lifts Rafa up so that my dear companion faces me with her. It's as if she has it in her mind to puppeteer with Rafa. That won't do! But before I can say so, my dear companion bares her needle-sharp teeth and squirms around.

"So sorry . . ." Alina blinks, moistening lashes, even as Rafa curls up on her lap. She fears I might deny her the privilege of tending to my dear companions. I wouldn't, not even when she does things that upset them. For I'm not tending them as well as I should either.

"It's all right," I lie, though the conditions of our imprisonment are inhuman for us, even worse for Rafa and Mufu. "But don't touch their feet. They're delicate."

"I won't!" Alina promises, hugging Rafa fiercely despite her low growl of protest. "I won't, I won't, I won't."

Worried. I'm as worried about my companions as I am about what will become of me and my sisters. Through our journey from the palace, through the narrow tunnels to the train station, and then onto this train, the six guards have remained the same. The women who serve us, however, change at every station. They might as well not change, for they're all the same: old widows with white hair braided tight, with lips sealed shut, with not a trace of kindness left in their wiry bodies, let alone compassion toward us. They serve us oat porridge for breakfast, rye bread and hard cheese for lunch, and mushy meat and vegetables for dinner. They empty our chamber pots when full, but never rinse them particularly clean. Thrice a day, they take Rafa and Mufu to the guards' day carriage, there to perform their business on old newspapers, I've been led to understand. When the train stops, they take my companions out for a quick walk. Fear. I always fear that they won't come back in time, that the train will continue onward with my companions abandoned alone in a desolate town.

I swallow to prevent myself from tearing up. I mustn't let Alina see me cry. But if I were to lose my dear companions, it would no doubt feel as bad as losing one of my sisters. I don't want to lose Rafa and Mufu. I don't want to lose Alina or Sibilia, or even Elise and Celestia. I don't want to be apart from Mama. Oh, Papa Moon, please let us be reunited with her soon!

"Merile . . ." Alina's voice drifts off as if she forgot what she was going to ask or as if she were listening to someone whispering at her. She twitches, then continues, "Why don't we ask Papa to turn us into deer?"

"Whh—what?" I'm so shocked by her question that when Mufu tugs at the hare leg, it falls from my hold and tumbles onto the carpet. Both Rafa and Mufu jump after it. They snarl playfully at each other, teeth bared, ears pulled back.

I study my sister, who seems so frail and small between the two plump cushions. Sometimes she acts strangely, speaks of shadows and treats objects as if they were alive. Has she somehow guessed what I was thinking, or is her question a mere coincidence?

"Or mice." A smile tugs at the corner of Alina's pale lips as she watches my companions fight over the hare leg. She giggles behind a raised palm. "They're so silly."

I smile with her. My darling dears are silly at times. And we're silly, too.

"What would be the point in that when there's no need to flee?" I ponder aloud, even though we are fleeing the Summer City, even though I have this feeling that we should abandon this train upon the first chance. Unrests haunt Mama's empire, and somehow Gagargi Prataslav is to blame for that. That night in the palace he ordered the guards to take us away. But Mama told us to go with them. Are they on our side or do they serve him? "The guards, Captain Janlav, are here to protect us."

"Please, don't mention his name."

Surprised by Elise taking part in the conversation, I swirl on the sofa to meet my sister's gaze. Her gray eyes are wide, and her freckled cheeks blush. She holds a needle up, poised to strike. Sequins glitter on the thread. That's no embroidery she's doing.

"Why?" I ask, because I want to know. Though the guards have remained the same throughout the journey, Captain Janlav is the only one I know by his real name. I remember him and Elise dancing at Alina's name day party. It's curious that he's now here with us, and that my sister doesn't want to hear of him.

"Yes, why would that be?" Sibilia chimes in from the divan by the window, opposite to Elise. She lowers the fountain pen and stares critically at her notes. How she can bear to study the scriptures, let alone ponder their meaning, completely escapes me. "For if I remember correctly . . ."

Red. Elise's cheeks glow red. The train shudders, and so do the teacups abandoned empty on the marble-topped table. When Elise speaks, her voice echoes this sound. "Because I asked you nicely."

Sibilia sighs and rolls her eyes, but she resumes reading the scriptures. I don't know how she can take this from our sister. We deserve to know; if not everything, then at least something.

"I want to know," I say, because Sibilia and Alina would never have the courage to ask for the truth. Rafa lifts her head as though I'd addressed her. Mufu uses this opening to steal the hare leg for herself. Defeated, Rafa jumps back onto Alina's sofa.

Elise glances at Celestia, lips drawn tight. Celestia lowers her needlework on her lap. She draws her shoulders back. She tilts her chin up, and her neck seems longer than it can possibly be. "Dear Merile, be glad that you don't know. Knowledge can be a very dangerous thing to possess. I ask you to trust your older sisters to guard you from any possible harm."

How dare she! But as she's the oldest of us, her word is final and there's no point in arguing against her. I mutter, "Glad. I'm so very, very glad that I know nothing at all."

Alina stares at me, eyes wide. Darkness lies under her eyes, in her gaze. How much does she really understand? Then she resumes petting Rafa as if we'd conversed about the weather or something equally boring. Of this, I'm glad indeed.

For a moment no one speaks. The only sound is Sibilia's pen scraping against the thick pages. She mutters under her breath, something I can't quite make out, but that might have been: "A day longer in this train, and we'll be clawing out each other's eyes."

"Come here," I call at Mufu. My dear companion glances at me, more interested in gnawing the hare leg on the floor than comforting me. That won't do. "Yes, here, my silly dear."

Mufu yaps at me, thin tail wagging. I meet her gaze and bare my teeth. She yaps once more before she jumps back on the sofa and trots onto my lap. Though her paws press painfully against my thighs, even through the itching woolen dress, I wrap my arms around her. Too much. Sibilia is right. We've spent too much time together during this horrid journey. Though the train consists of a locomotive and four carriages, we're allowed only in two. At night we toss and turn in our own separate cabins, crammed things better suited for servants. Each morning, we're herded into this carriage. Though the train stops almost daily, we haven't been allowed out even once, not even to take Rafa and Mufu out!

I miss the smell of snow and open skies. I miss . . .

"I've thought it through," Alina says cheerily. Rafa's pink tongue lolls out of her mouth as if she already knew what my sister is about to say.

I glance at my sister from under my brows, wary. This morning, she wouldn't touch her blackcurrant juice. I managed to coach her into tasting a spoonful, but she wouldn't drink more. During lunch, she drank only half of her tea. It's as if she knew it was spiked.

"What exactly have you thought through?" I ask. When Alina evades her medicine, her mind wanders to strange places, and the things she says frighten me more than I care to admit.

"Last night, when I waited for the shadows, I went through all the animals I know," Alina gushes. Both Rafa and Mufu stare at her, eyes wide, ears spread wide. I hear Celestia and Elise perching on their seat—the springs in the chairs squeak when they move. "A deer would be so fast that the red-gloves couldn't hit me with their rifles. Though a deer might not be able to sneak out of the train, and I might injure myself upon jumping out."

"Then it sounds like Papa shouldn't turn us into deer," I reply, too weary to tell her to stop, too weary of this journey that seems to never end. The guards haven't told us where we're going. "To safety, Mama said," Celestia repeats time after time. I miss Mama. Papa Moon, can you tell her that when you shine upon her? I'm sure she already worries about what became of us!

"That's what I thought, too. Now, a mouse is smaller. And nimbler. I think I could hide from the owls and hawks, in snow tunnels or in hollow logs."

I pretend to merely shift into a more comfortable position, but actually glance at Celestia. The sideways tilt of her chin reveals she's listening, though she continues her mysterious sewing. She must have thought of fleeing too. She might be thinking about it at this very moment.

"What about a dog?" I ask, though I shouldn't entertain Alina's ideas. Many things are in Papa's power, but turning people into animals happens only in stories. Yet, it can't hurt to give her hope. Even if there's some, Celestia refused to give us any, though she must have a plan. She's the one who'll marry the Moon one day and become the empress after Mama!

The plan. I want so badly to ask her about the plan, but I don't dare to bring up the topic. Though the guards spend the days in their own day carriage, playing cards and smoking, they're never far away. We can hear the jagged echoes of their jesting, which means they might be able to hear us too. And there's always a guard positioned behind the locked door leading to our sleeping carriage.

"That might work." Alina nods to herself, and Rafa nods with her. Though not as if she were agreeing, but in a way that states she's hoping my little sister will eventually slip her a treat. "If Papa were to turn us into such fine dogs as Rafa and Mufu, I'm sure no one could catch us."

Ridiculous. It's a ridiculous idea, of course. But I decide to entertain Alina. Her eyelids seem heavier now. Let her fall asleep while thinking of my companions, not the night we had to leave home. "They have been bred for speed . . ."

"But their coats are so very thin." Alina yawns. She giggles at herself, for failing to cover her mouth with her palm. She tugs the hem of her dress around Rafa. My companion doesn't mind. "We'd need coats."

My cloak. I shuffle out of my fur-lined cloak, the one my seed gave me what feels like so long ago. I miss him, though even when I was free, we didn't see each other that often. Where is he now? Why is no one helping us? Where is Celestia's seed, the great one-eyed General Monzanov? Where is the mighty General Kravakiv that Mama favored twice? Is Alina's seed still in the south?

Unease swells in my throat. The Poet, even if he does care about me, about us, as much as he claims, he'd be powerless to help. A pen is no weapon against a man as twisted as Gagargi Prataslav.

"Coats..." Alina yawns once more. She keels over on the sofa. Rafa curls next to her. My sister wraps her twiggy arms around her. "I feel so sleepy."

"Sleep," I say, carefully pushing myself up from the sofa. Though it's been months already since I sprained my left ankle, a dull ache climbs up my leg. I hide the pain the best I can as I shuffle to Alina. I blanket her with my cloak to keep her warm, and sit beside her. I'm not sure she sleeps during the nights. Though Celestia has requested so on multiple occasions, we're not allowed to share the cabins. If that doesn't make us prisoners, then what will? "You should sleep."

Alina smiles as Mufu jumps onto her sofa. My companion curls on top of her feet. I reposition the cloak so that only her black nose peeks out. Alina closes her eyes, and her breathing deepens. I wait by her side patiently. She might not have consumed the full portion of her medicine, but once she does fall asleep, the dream is thick and lasts long. Thank the Moon for that!

Once I'm sure Alina is asleep, I leave her in the care of my companions and approach my sisters. It's curious how soon we found our own places in this carriage. Alina and I always sit on the same sofas, the ones by the door that leads to the cloakroom and then into the guards' day carriage. Celestia, Elise, and Sibilia always remain by the oval dining table, the oldest on the heavily padded chairs, Sibilia on the divan by the window. Routine. I guess it's a routine of sorts.

"She's asleep, then?" Sibilia pauses her scribbling and glances up at me. Her hands bear ink stains. Some of them are more than a day old.

I really miss bathing. In this train, we must clean ourselves with small towels and a bowl of lukewarm water that the servant brings with her each morning. "Safe and sound with Rafa and Mufu."

"Good for her," Sibilia mutters. There's more she wants to say, but won't. It annoys me nevertheless. Behave. At least I know how to behave, even in these most trying circumstances. I merely sway my hem in protest as I limp past Celestia and Elise to the silver samovar perched on the cupboard to the right of the door.

Cold. The white porcelain cup is cold. I pour myself a thick layer of the golden zavarka tea. I inhale the malty, smoky scent before I draw steaming water for myself. It's drafty in the carriage, but Alina needs my cloak more than I do, for she won't sleep well if she's cold. I poke at the sugar with a silver spoon. Humidity has turned it lumpy. I'd never known that sort of thing could happen.

I limp back with the cup, careful not to spill, as the train sways in that unpredictable way that is in its nature. I take the last free seat, the one at the end of the oval table, and cradle the cup in my hands. But before I can taste the tea, Sibilia crawls to the far end of the divan. "Ugh, you stink of the rats."

Drop. Can she just not let it drop? Apparently not. I growl at her, "You stink."

Elise glares at both of us, scissors glimmering in the light of the osprey chandelier. I sip my tea to prevent myself from saying words I might later regret. Though our meals are bland, apparently the same as those that the guards and servants eat, the tea is of the imperial brand. It reminds me of home, of the days when we could go wherever we pleased, of the days when I could take my companions on long walks in the gardens, of days when they didn't have to pee indoors.

"Whatever," Sibilia sighs, turning a page loudly as if what she'd read had somehow offended her. But that's all for show.

I set the cup down on the saucer with a clink. How dare she continue insulting me! "Unfair. You're so very unfair. It wasn't Rafa's fault! You should look where you step!"

"Your rat peed on the carpet." Sibilia glares at me from over the book, then looks pointedly at the slightly yellow spot at the exact center of the thick white carpet covering the carriage's floor.

"She was frightened and confused," I hiss back at her. We were all frightened and confused during the first days! I bet that if it had been I who'd had the accident, my sister would have already forgiven and forgotten it.

"Enough," Celestia says, waving curtly at us. The movement is strange, like a broken wing's flap, and she seems equally confused by it. "Sibilia, no permanent harm was done. Shoes and socks can be washed."

"Thank you." I beam at Celestia. That will teach Sibilia to insult my dear companions!

"Merile—" Celestia turns her full attention to me, and how I hate her for doing so. For hers is a gaze as blue as the skies we haven't seen in days. Hers is the skill in disapproval that almost rivals that of Nurse Nookes. No, one that surpasses that by a wide berth. "We are in this train together. Try not to get insulted over every single little thing. Try to remember that other people might get equally upset about something you say or do."

Blaming. Now she's blaming me. She's not on my side after all! "I'm not getting mad over everything. I haven't done anything wrong."

"Point proven." Sibilia clasps the book of scriptures shut.

"Stop it," Elise says. "Both of you."

I stick my tongue out at them. Then I sip my tea in a sullen silence for what feels like hours, but could very well be mere minutes. Slowly, it gets darker. Though the curtains are drawn shut, evening enters the carriage. It's dark and bleak.

"My fingers hurt," Elise says at last, dropping her needlework on the table. She pushes it away from her. It's only then that I realize what she was working on. It's a sleeve of the ball gown she wore the night we boarded the train, and she's removed half of the sequins and beads already. "And my back cramps."

Celestia merely glances up at Elise from her own needlework. The thread she works coils heavy on her lap. She slips another sequin onto the string. I recognize the beads and sequins. They're from Elise's dress, too.

"Why are you destroying the dress?" I ask. And why Elise's dress and not the one Celestia wore? Does this imply my oldest sister thinks that she might still need it later?

"We aren't destroying it," Elise replies, even as the proof lies there before her, on the table. "We are altering it."

How dare she lie to me! Altering means taking in a seam or adding more pearls in the neckline. The two of them are dismantling the most beautiful of Elise's ball gowns. Why would they do so when all we have to wear are the plain woolen dresses that no one even washes for us?

"Stop treating me like a child," I snap at them. "You two have a plan. I want to know what it is!"

Celestia shakes her head as if she were disappointed in me, and that does feel more horrible than any evil thing Sibilia has ever said about my companions. But it's Elise who speaks. "Dear Merile, you are eleven. As far as I'm concerned, that falls within the definition of a child. And as far as your behavior is concerned, you still act very much like one."

I push myself up from the chair. Pain. Pain lances through my left leg. I pick up the empty teacup and weigh it in my hand. Only Celestia's sad expression, the promise of utter disappointment, keeps me from tossing the cup at Elise. I slam it against the plate.

"Merile." Celestia addresses me very, very sternly.

I can't bear to face her, and so I stare down at the cup. As I shift my hand, the gilded handle remains around my forefinger like a ring. Did I really break the cup?

"Stop it. Stop it now," I shriek, tugging at the ear. It won't come off. "Stop pretending like I'm not present. Tell me what's really happening!"

My voice lashes through the dim carriage, undampened by the curtains. Rafa and Mufu stir under my cloak. I realize only then how loud my voice must have been. I stare back at them, praying I haven't woken up little Alina. Her eyes stay closed. Bless Papa Moon!

Clatter. Clatter of boots comes from the direction of the guards' day carriage.

"Quick," Elise whispers to Celestia even as she snatches her needlework from the table and promptly sits on top of it. "They are coming."

Celestia stares at the door, akin to a deer who has heard a hunter's horn blown. She quickly loops the sequined thread around her hand. The thread is very long. It will take her too long to hide it.

Squeal of a key turning in the lock. My gaze darts from the door to little Alina. She sleeps unknowing of everything under my cloak, on the sofa closest to the door. Abandoned. I feel like I've abandoned her in a storm of my own making.

Celestia tugs the thread under her hem just as the door swings open. The scissors remain on the table. She doesn't have time to hide them.

"What's happening here?" Captain Janlav strides in, his midnight blue coat halfway donned, gripping a rifle. He doesn't have his hat on, and his brown topknot is hastily tied. His jaw muscles are tense as if he's come prepared for a battle.

"Nothing," I reply before I realize that's the most condemning thing I could have possibly said. I don't have to look at my older sisters to sense their utter disappointment in me.

Captain Janlav takes in the scene with military precision, and I'm sure no detail can escape him. He doesn't find anything amiss with the sleeping Alina, nor Sibilia, who clutches the book of scriptures against her chest. We've been provided with the needles and scissors so that we can darn our clothes—the servants won't do even that for us—and seeing them on the table doesn't alarm him. Gradually, his hold on the rifle relaxes, but he doesn't loop the strap around his shoulder.

"I ..." Shame stings my tongue. I brought his attention upon us. If Celestia and Elise really have a plan, for the time being we need to appear harmless and subdued. At risk. I've placed my sisters at risk. Why under the Moon did I do so?

"Yes?" Captain Janlav asks, and I'm still not sure what he thinks of us. His brown eyes reveal nothing. Not whether he's alarmed or amused by us.

"I broke a cup," I mutter, flush-faced. Then inspiration strikes me. I point a blaming finger at Elise. The teacup's separated ear glints under the light of the slowly swinging chandelier. "She called me a child!"

Captain Janlav drifts three steps toward my sister, past the sofa where Alina sleeps. He looks Elise in the eye. There's something in that gaze. Not recognition, but . . . I don't know what to call it. Though he's served my family for years, though he betrayed us, it's as if he constantly keeps on forgetting who my sister is.

"Captain Janlav." Elise nods at him. She should get up from the chair, properly greet him. But she can't, not when she's sitting on top of the disassembled sleeve. Why did I have to point him in her direction? Fool. What a fool I was!

"You must understand . . ." Elise smiles at him in the way she does when she wants people to think that obeying her was their own idea. "Sometimes Merile acts rash. She's only eleven, after all."

Captain Janlav's eyelids droop. It's as if he's hearing the sweetest music, as if he's seeing the most beautiful of sights. And yet, at the same time, it's as if he's forgetting everything Elise has ever said to him, including the very words he must have just heard. "I . . ."

"Can you tell the servant to bring us dinner?" Celestia asks, as if we'd summoned him here for that very purpose. "I believe it is the time soon."

Captain Janlav nods curtly at her. He swirls around, heels clicking together, and returns to the door leading to the cloakroom. The thick carpeting muffles his passage. When he closes the door, he does so softly and carefully, as if not to frighten us with the sound.

Elise springs up from the chair as if a needle had stung her in the very backside. She paces the length of the carriage, rubbing her temple with both hands. "It's as if he has never seen me before." She turns at the door, strides back to Celestia. "Is it really within the gagargi's power to make a man forget love?"

Celestia glances at Sibilia and me. She doesn't reply a word. So little. Elise has said so little, and yet too much, I sense.

Once Elise loved Captain Janlav. What this means, I really don't know.

Chapter 8

Sibilia

Hello, Scribs.

Yes, it's still just plain hello for you. "Dear" is a precious title that you must earn by listening to my secrets and guarding them. We've known each other for three weeks only. That's quite many days, and yet not that many at all. Dear Notes, whom I miss so very much, was my companion and confidante for two years, seven months, and eleven days, ever since I started keeping a diary.

I don't know you well enough yet to trust you, and you can't know me that well either. Perhaps you can tell from my handwriting which days have been good and which beyond terrible. See how scrawny and shaky, borderline unreadable, my handwriting is now? There's no need to remark on that. It's been such an awful two days that, to begin with, I don't even want to write about them. But I suspect that writing might make me feel better, and at this point I'm willing to resort to absolutely anything.

By the way, Scribs. This dialog with you, it doesn't flow naturally yet. It's not fair of me to continually compare you to Notes. I must give you a chance to prove your worth. Very well then. Here goes.

Argh. Why is this so difficult? Scribs, a little help here would be much appreciated!

Yesterday, after the silent servant departed with the lunch dishes, I immersed myself in the exciting world of the scriptures, as has become my habit. Yes, Scribs, contrary to what you might think, I do read the scriptures before I write sideways over them. It's not exactly my fault that I had to abandon Notes that night the guards escorted us to the train with me wearing nothing but my nightgown (and since thinking of that still makes me want to die of shame, from now on we shall simply pretend that it never happened). It's curious that there are no notebooks or letter paper on this train, but that the guards forgot to unclip this fountain pen from your side. Then again, there are many things I don't understand when it comes to this journey's peculiar arrangements. For example, we have only one hairbrush and comb between the five of us—and since Merile so kindly decided to steal the brush for her rats, the rest of us have to do with one comb. One. Comb.

My head started to ache after an hour or so, and I simply couldn't continue reading. I closed my eyes and tried to dream of K, of how he'd gallop to our rescue, and then sweep me up in his arms. Well, I dreamed of more than that, but those thoughts are so intimate that I don't feel comfortable sharing them with you. Not yet in any case.

It was then that I heard the strange conversation between Merile and Alina. No, I wasn't eavesdropping. As such. There's just no privacy to be had when you're forced to share one carriage with your sisters every single day. We're lucky, though, to have our own cabins for the nights. I can't imagine having to share a room with any one of them. Don't get me wrong, Scribs, I love my sisters above anything else. But there's a limit to how long I can listen to Celestia's rational reasoning, Elise pining after that captain who's clearly forgotten everything about her, or worse, talking of how the revolution isn't necessarily a bad thing. And Merile, dear Papa help me, she either throws hissy fits or prattles on about her rats that pee on the carpets and poo on the floor (well, perhaps the latter hasn't yet happened, but it's only a matter of time, if you ask me). But even so, the worst is Alina, because sometimes her mind wanders down paths that lead to unsettling places.

So what did she say today? I'll tell you, Scribs. Have just a little more patience.

Merile and Alina were feeding the rats dried hare legs once more. The rats gnawed at the leather and bones, silent enough. Merile cooed over the rats as if they were the most perfect creatures ever to live. But Alina wouldn't say a word, no matter how Merile coached her.

"What is it?" Merile finally asked.

Every one of us is concerned about Alina. More often than not, she leaves her meals untouched. Since we don't know what she'll taste, we'll have to spike everything with her medicine: the porridge, the eye of butter, the cloudberry jam, the blackcurrant juice, and her tea. This is something our captors didn't foresee, and we're now running out of the supply. Based on the discussions Celestia has had with Captain Janlav, Alina's medicine isn't something that's easily acquired here in the middle of nowhere.

Alina buried her head against the brown rat's back. I really had to hearken my senses to make out her words. But this is what she said: "I fear something has happened to Mama."

I think Merile has an inkling of what really came to pass, though Celestia and Elise won't talk of it for fear of upsetting Alina. Try as we may to keep secrets from each other, there's no way to hide the truth when we breathe the same air day af-

154 • Leena Likitalo

ter day. And lately, that air has been getting very stale indeed. Up till yesterday evening, we hadn't been let out even once.

"Mama." Merile sniffed, but her hold on the bone loosened so much that the black rat managed to snatch it for itself. I don't know if she does it on purpose, but things have been slipping from her fingers more and more often lately. "Mama is the Crescent Empress. No harm can fall on her under the Moon."

No matter how annoying Merile sometimes acts, I do admire her bravery. She knows her duty without having to be told. We must hold up the façade before Alina, for to her, ignorance is bliss. For a long time, I wanted to be older, but now I would like to be younger. Much younger. Too young to understand that Gagargi Prataslav's schemes have torn Mama's empire asunder.

Instead of being soothed by Merile's words, Alina sank deeper into the sofa, taking the brown rat with her. Though her eyes are deep set, with perpetual dark circles around them, her gaze was strong and unwavering. Un-ignorable. One by one, Celestia, Elise, I, and Merile lowered our needles and teacups and whatnots and turned to face our little sister.

"A shadow of a swan visited me last night," she said in a gossamer-thin, trembling voice. She clutched the brown rat against her chest. "Mama is dead."

Celestia paled. She breathed rapidly through her mouth the denial every single one of us wanted to voice. "No . . ."

Elise clasped a hand over her mouth. "Surely . . ."

"A swan?" I asked, trying to make sense of what I'd heard. If Alina had been visited by our family's charge, the most sacred bird . . . The scriptures say many things about swans, some truly terrifying when you stop to think about them.

"A shadow," Merile repeated. This meant more to her. There

was something Alina hadn't shared with the rest of us, and I couldn't figure it out then.

"It couldn't keep her safe . . ." Alina burst into tears then. The brown rat on her lap turned around, whip-fast, to lick her face. That did little to soothe her. She only wailed louder. "Mama is dead!"

The wail battered against the lacquered wood panels, echoed through the length of the carriage. At once, Celestia was on her feet, and Elise too. I scooted after them, always clumsier and slower. Mama had decided to remain behind in the Summer City. She'd sent us away with the guards to keep us safe. But that wasn't the whole story. We aren't free to come and go as we please—we're prisoners here.

"Now, now . . ." Celestia kneeled before the sofa, cupping Alina's tear-stained cheeks with her slender hands. Her voice, when she spoke, was so ethereal and kind that I wanted to believe her too. "It was just a bad dream."

Alina paused her bawling only to draw a shuddering breath. "No. Not a dream. I sheltered that shadow in my hem."

The rat that had lain on Merile's lap jumped down and rushed to lick Alina's hands. Merile dashed after it to Alina's left side. Elise settled on the other side. Uncertain of what to do or how to help, I hovered behind Celestia.

"Hush, now," Celestia tried. There was one thing she'd said from the very beginning, one rule we had to adhere to, no matter how challenging it felt at times. We should never draw attention to ourselves. We had to wear the simple dresses we were told to wear. We had to eat the meager meals without a single complaint voiced. We had to establish a routine so that the guards would forget that we existed and when the time came for us to break the routine, it would take them longer to notice that. "Hush now, my little Alina."

A series of trembles traveled from the tip of Alina's head all the way to her tiny feet. "It wasn't a dream," she cried. "The swan told me. Mama is dead!"

If anything, her voice had gotten just louder! It chimed against the curtained windows, scattered from the osprey chandelier. I met Elise's eyes by chance, and her expression mirrored my dread. This wasn't good.

"Mama! Mama . . ."

But if there's one positive thing to be said about Merile's temper tantrums, it's that the guards have grown as weary of them as we have. And yet, we couldn't count on them not coming to investigate this disturbance. Eventually, they'd come.

"What do we do?" A part of me did believe Alina. Not a big part, but swans are sacred. If Mama were dead, if the guards learned that we knew of it, they'd want to know how we'd acquired this information. They would search through our cabins and carriages. Celestia's master plan would no doubt be thwarted.

The same thought must have crossed Elise's mind, for she muttered the most unbecoming curses under her breath. Where she'd learned such peasant manners, I can but wonder.

"Don't say a word." Celestia cast a warning look at us. She took a deep breath and met Alina's gaze. "Hush now, we heard you. You fear for Mother."

I nodded, but in my mind, I wondered if shocked little Alina had even registered Celestia's words.

It was then that we heard the pounding of boots in the cloakroom. Soon after, the door opened and Captain Janlav entered the carriage. His midnight blue coat was buttoned all the way up, but it was missing two silver buttons. He didn't wear a hat, and the once-shaved sides of his head grew short brown hair. His rifle rested against his back, and he didn't seem inclined to unstrap it.

"What is going on here this time around?" He actually sighed.

Elise got up from her seat, elegantly, like a dove taking to the air. She circled the sofa that Merile had occupied earlier and smoothed her skirts in a way that promised she'd take care of the captain, no matter what that would require. Though now that he seemed bored to begin with, a kind smile from my sister might suffice.

I still didn't know what to do. Just hover behind Celestia? I felt out of place, someone whose mere presence would call forth suspicion. I quickly stole Elise's place on the sofa and hugged little Alina. At least she no longer wailed, merely sobbed. But her sobbing did wring my heartstrings.

"Captain Janlav," Elise said, halting before the guard. She leaned toward him, her head angled minutely so that she could study him from under her red-gold brows. "That's your name, soldier, isn't it?"

For a moment, Captain Janlav stared at Elise as though he'd never met her before, in awe as if she were the most beautiful girl in this world. Which she may well be. His chapped lips parted. He closed his eyes. A shudder ran through his body. When he opened his eyes, he pointedly avoided looking at Elise, but gazed past her at us.

Oh, Scribs, how we must have looked to him! Girls with dirty, braided hair. White dresses no longer pristine, but stinking of sweat and stained at the hem and sleeves. Skin oily and flaking at the same time. All of us red-cheeked. One sobbing, the others distraught by this. It makes me want to cry when I think of what has become of us.

"Yes," Captain Janlav replied to Elise at last. Sometimes I think even he doesn't know what he's doing. Perhaps he didn't realize what it would be like to keep another human being as a captive for weeks. Perhaps it's as painful for him to keep us locked in the carriage as it is for us to be so confined. I wonder ... No, I'm sure he doesn't know what the gagargi is hoping to accomplish. But he must know where we're heading. Can it be worse there than it is here?

Elise circled the captain so that if he wanted to address her, he'd need to do so with his back against us. She glanced past him, at us, with one eyebrow cocked. From that I gathered that she wanted Alina distracted. I pressed my hands over our little sister's ears as if we were about to play some silly game. Celestia caught my intention and made a funny face at her. Since when has the empress-to-be known how to do such!

"Our little sister ..." Elise offered the captain a girlish shrug, one that spoke of embarrassment, but also positioned her assets in the most flattering angle. This too, had to be something she'd practiced before her mirrors. If you must know, Scribs, I haven't touched my hand mirror since we boarded this train, but seeing my sister utilize her skills renewed my resolve to practice mine. "You know of her condition."

Captain Janlav's posture betrayed nothing of what he might have been thinking. Our little sister's weakness was a secret, but not a particularly well-kept one. Since our captors had had the foresight to pack with them her medicine, they had to know of it. "Yes. I'm aware of it."

I did wonder then if he'd ever been capable of forming full sentences. Once upon a time, Elise had danced with this man. She claimed she'd kissed him on multiple occasions, that they'd been in love. But now, he acted as if they'd never met. Or if they had, it was on the night that he'd escorted us into this train, and that was it.

"She's not eating or sleeping," Elise said, every word the truth. "There has been a turn for the worse in her condition."

Captain Janlav glanced over his shoulder, brown eyes narrowing. He isn't a stupid man; the opposite. He could sense something was afoot.

Elise reached out to grab his arm, but he strode to us, too fast for her to stop him. Despite his determination, he moved silently, akin to a hunter. The carpet must have dulled the thud of his boots.

As he approached, Celestia, Elise, I, and Merile stared at him in a horror of sorts. If he'd ask Alina what ailed her, she'd tell. That much was for sure. I could already see it, the guards turning over every pillow and blanket, finding you, Scribs, and the pearl bracelets Celestia had made. They'd confiscate them and keep us locked in our cabins. Day and night through. We'd never see the sky again.

Captain Janlav halted behind Celestia. He motioned for me to remove my hands from over Alina's ears. I did so hastily, hoping he wouldn't notice how much they trembled.

"Well then, little one, what is it that has so unsettled you?" It was the kindness in his voice I hadn't expected. He was our captor. I wanted to think of him as an evil man. But that he is not.

Alina's colorless lips parted. Her tiny teeth peeked out. She blinked as if she were not quite sure where she was, and with whom.

I prayed to Papa for her to not say it, for anything else to happen. Anything at all . . . Oh, Scribs, that's exactly what happened.

Alina spasmed. Her back arched violently, and her head lolled uncontrollably. She squealed a disquieting sound, something an injured animal might shriek. I shrank away from her, fearing I'd caused the spasm, by asking Papa for help. But now that I think of it, it can't have been that, but rather the shock of finding Captain Janlav there, looming over her.

I did burst into tears, and so did Merile. But Captain Janlav brushed Celestia aside briskly and kneeled before Alina. "Hold her still."

Elise took my place. Celestia replaced Merile at Alina's side. They clamped their hands around our little sister's arms.

"Do hold her still," Captain Janlav repeated calmly, as if he'd seen the worst things that can come to pass in life. Well, he's a soldier. Perhaps he has. "Hold her head still."

Elise pressed her body against Alina's, pinning our little sister against the sofa. Celestia cupped her head. Captain Janlav bent over her.

"You must not let her move," Captain Janlav said, and then, without waiting for further acknowledgement, he pried little Alina's lids up, one at a time.

Only the whites of her eyes showed. His lips pressed into a tight line. I don't know what he'd expected to see. Us using our little sister as a ruse? Could he really think that ill of us?

Alina spasmed again, so forcefully I feared her back would snap. It was at that horrifying moment that two more guards stormed into our carriage. One was the big burly man with a protruding belly. We don't know his name, but I've named him Belly. The other was gnarly and narrow, even younger than Captain Janlav. Him, I've named Boy.

"What are they up to this time around?" Belly brandished a rifle as if he'd had it in his mind to teach us a lesson.

"Can't you see?" Captain Janlav shouted back at him. He pressed Alina's shoulders, to keep her down. A wet spot appeared on her lap. My poor sister had lost control of her bladder.

Belly and Boy glanced at each other. Boy looked as if he were about to snigger or make a distasteful remark.

"Close the door," Captain Janlav growled at them. "Wait outside. That's a direct order from me, and thus from the gagargi himself."

Belly and Boy paled. Belly fumbled with his rifle as if guns could solve anything, least of all heal my sister. Boy grabbed his arm and led the older man out. But even as the door clicked shut, Alina kept on spasming.

"Is there anyone with medical skills aboard?" Celestia asked. The Moon bless us that she's the empress-to-be, rational even in the most distressing of situations!

Captain Janlav shook his head, worry etching chasms on his forehead. "No."

It was then that the full meaning of the words he'd said to Belly and Boy dawned upon me. He's in charge of this operation and, it seems, also of our safety. If anything were to happen to us, Gagargi Prataslav would hold him accountable for that.

"We must . . ." Elise paused to swallow a sob. Her gray eyes were doe-wide, pleading. "We must get her help."

But just as suddenly as Alina had started spasming, she stilled. No, that's not the right word. She collapsed onto the sofa as if she had not a single strand of strength left in her body. Her narrow chest sank with a shuddering exhale. Then her breathing resumed a shallow rhythm. Her eyes remained closed.

"We will get her help," Captain Janlav said. He squeezed Elise's shoulder in a way that might have been just a reflex or then meant something much more. Then he left without as much as looking over his shoulder.

Scribs, it was truly terrible. Almost the most terrible thing I've ever witnessed! The scriptures, yes you know it, I've been reading them because there isn't anything else to read here. And though I might have once claimed so to dear Notes, I don't know them by heart. I hardly ever bothered to read a full chapter before. But there's one sentence that brought me comfort as I repeated it in my mind.

After all the wrong, there will be right.
After all the wrong, there will be right.
After all the wrong, there will be right.

The day passed slowly as my sisters and I patted Alina's forehead with a cold, wet cloth and massaged her arms and legs. The nameless servant woman came to clean, but she couldn't quite scrub off the yellow stain on the sofa. She helped us change Alina's dress. She eyed our little sister, radiating pity, and then spoke the first words we'd ever heard from her, or any of the other servants, for that matter. She offered to spoon honeyed tea into Alina's mouth. We told her not to bother, since Alina would spit it out. And then we tried that ourselves, in the hopes that it might revive her.

It didn't, and the servant left soon after, no doubt to report this turn of events to Captain Janlav.

Eventually, when the day turned blue, the train's speed decelerated. I felt tempted to run to the door and bang on it with my bare fists. Though we've stopped at numerous stations during the journey, we've never been let out. Celestia said early on that we shouldn't let people know our identity. Mama's empire is still infested with unrests, and many vehemently hate anyone with noble blood in their veins. There are people out there who are ready to harm us just for who we are, in ways that I don't want to think about (though sometimes when I lie alone in my cabin, I do, and then I feel cold inside and can't sleep for hours), even if we've played no part in what has so angered them. Curious as it is, as long as we remain in the train, we're safe.

But now Alina . . . my poor little sister was ill. She needed help, and that help wasn't available in the train.

The train halted in a small town, or it might have been a village—Elise peeked through the crack between the curtains to report this. We listened to the sounds of the train being fueled and watered. And then, after what felt like ages, rather than hearing the train rattle into motion, we heard the key turn in the lock of the cloakroom's door. The servant entered without as much as a knock. Boy tramped in after her, without as much as a greeting. They strode through the carriage, to the door leading to our cabins, and out.

"I wonder what that was about," Merile muttered.

I was too tired to even think about it.

It didn't take long for us to find out. The servant and Boy returned with the blankets that barely kept us warm during the nights. Captain Janlav entered the carriage almost at the exact same moment.

"Wrap into the blankets," Captain Janlav ordered. Then he marched to the sofa, where Alina still lay wrapped in Merile's fur cloak. He lifted her up as if she weighed nothing at all. Celestia hastened to tug the cloak better around our sister. He shrugged her aside. "Follow me. Say not a word. Run not a step."

Those were the conditions we had to agree to. It wasn't a hard choice for us. We wanted to help Alina more than anything else in the world.

We donned the blankets as cloaks and rushed after him like animals released from a cage. Our freedom was short-lived, however. As soon as we stepped out of the train, the four remaining guards, the ones that always stink of liquor and cigarettes, formed lines on both our sides. Boy held the back.

I didn't care. I was ecstatic to walk under the open sky once more. The day was just about to yield to the night, and everything was of that particular shade of blue that not even the most talented artists can quite capture. The clouds, the snowfields, the shadows bore the blue veil proudly. The freezing cold air stung my nostrils, tickled my lungs. Yet I puffed white clouds in excitement. For at that moment I remembered what it felt like to be free.

The town was small. A dozen or so two-story log buildings loomed over the main street. There was just enough space for my sisters and me on the path that the townspeople had trampled during the day. Fresh snow crunched under the guards' boots—they had to walk through the snow banks. We must have made a strange sight: Captain Janlav carrying my sister, four girls wrapped in gray blankets, akin to ghosts in the falling darkness, guarded by soldiers who might pass as our shadows.

We neither saw nor encountered anyone as we walked to the end of the main street. There, we took a lane to the right and continued a bit farther. At first, I didn't see the cottage. The town had no streetlights, which wasn't that surprising, since we hadn't sped through a city in a week.

I wanted to ask if this was where the doctor lived, but then I remembered Captain Janlav's instructions (which had sounded more like a warning to me) and bit my tongue instead. The same thought must have crossed Merile's mind, for she and her rats trod on my hem. When I glared at her from over my shoulder, the question was writ across her brown face.

Since Captain Janlav was carrying Alina, he wasn't the one to pound on the door. Beard was. As his red-gloved fist landed against the thick planks, it felt like an omen, and that made me think of Nurse Nookes, whom I'd sometimes called a witch, though she most certainly wasn't one.

But perhaps it was witchcraft that I happened to think of her just then. I kid you not here, Scribs. You'll believe me when I describe to you the strange events that unfolded next.

The door opened, but no one waited behind it. An aroma of crushed nettles and garlic gasped against us, so thick I could taste it. Captain Janlav stepped in without hesitation, Celestia at his heels. Elise made sure to tag along so close after her that no guard could slip in between, and I and Merile did likewise. Then the small cottage was already so full that the remaining guards didn't dare to squeeze in.

"Fire. I shall warm myself by the fire!" Merile limped to the fireplace, where a black kettle boiled above glowing embers. Her rats trotted after her as if nothing else mattered. As if they were right at home in the cottage.

My eyes took a while to get accustomed to the dark interior. I first felt the bunches of dried herbs and feathers brush against my head rather than saw them. A crude table occupied most of the room. Jars and glass bottles lay scattered on the wide planks. There was a small alcove at the back of the room. A woman emerged from there.

"Honored midwife, the little one has taken ill." Captain Janlav wagered a step toward the woman.

The old woman halted before him. A shawl as black as an old crow's feathers drooped against her hunched back. Her gray hair rested against the nape of her neck, in a knot that I doubted could be undone. Age emphasized her features, the beaky nose and beady eyes that a milky veil of blindness shrouded. Her blue-tinted lips drooped against her teeth so that I could easily distinguish the shape of each. She glanced at Alina, then past me at the open door and the guards there. No, not quite at her or the guards, but at their feet. She croaked, "Close door."

Beard met Captain Janlav's eyes from across the room. The captain nodded curtly. The soldier instantly obeyed. From this exchange I deduced that both of them were (and still are) desperate to keep my sisters and me safe, if you can believe that, Scribs. But about that we can debate later. Let me tell you what came to pass now before I stop believing it myself.

Once the cottage's door creaked shut, with the guards remaining outside, the old woman turned her full attention to us. At first I didn't understand what she was looking at—our uncomfortable sabots or the snow we'd brought in. Then it struck me. Though blind, she was, quite impossibly, studying our shadows.

"You say honored midwife . . ." The old woman spat on the gnarled plank floor. She stamped her sturdy boot over the phlegm and swirled it as if to put out a cigarette. "Bah! Say as it be or me no help."

Captain Janlav glanced at Celestia, then Elise. The corner of his mouth twitched, as did his moustache. There was indecision in him. Desperation, too. "Very well. I'll say it."

The old woman stared at him, her blind gaze bright with wisdom and age. In the light of the embers, it seemed to me that her black clothes shimmered and took on strange hues, red and yellow of autumn, those of glorious decay. Though I've worn the most luxurious of clothes myself, I've never seen any fabric behave in that way.

"Help the little one," Captain Janlav said, "Witch at the End of the Lane."

I gasped, for as soon as he named her, it all made sense. The cottage I hadn't at first noticed, the old woman's strange demeanor, his hesitation before her. My sisters and I, we'd been brought to a place of darkness, and danger, even. Celestia's shoulders drew back as if she were about to speak, but of what, I couldn't even begin to guess.

The witch waved my eldest sister quiet, barely missing a bouquet of herbs tied to dry from the low ceiling beam running across the length of the cottage. She was more commanding than my sister, the one who would be the empress sooner than any one of us could have predicted. Oh, Mama . . . No, I won't think of that. I will write of the witch.

"No talk. Me look." The witch hustled to the other side of the table and swept the bottles and jars aside. She motioned Captain Janlav to lower Alina. He didn't move, not till he received a nod from Celestia. As frail and young as our sister is, she fit on the cleared table with space to spare.

The witch gazed beside Alina, at the shadow that folded itself on Merile's white cloak. Her grin revealed the gaps between her crooked teeth. Then she gestured at the door, her words aimed at Captain Janlav. "Now you go out."

Captain Janlav's shoulders hitched up. His hands curled into fists as if he could only barely refrain from unstrapping his rifle and aiming it at the witch. "It's my responsibility to . . ."

The witch cut the air like a bird's wing strikes. Her almost see-through sleeve shifted about her arm long after the movement itself had ceased.

"You here. No help. Matters with woman's body." The witch traced with her finger the shadow of our little sister. "Even girl's. No cure when men present."

Captain Janlav's jaw set hard and his brows knit tight. I could almost sense what he was thinking. Alina needed help that no one but the witch could offer. My sisters and I were his responsibility, his prisoners. Would we tell the witch of our distress? What could she do to help us? Could we escape through the tiny windows behind the table? No, they were too small. Was there a back door? No, none at all.

"Very well then," he grunted, the corner of his mouth twitching. "I'll wait outside. But if I hear anything alarming, my men and I shall storm in, with drawn swords and loaded rifles."

The witch smiled in a self-satisfied, smug manner as the captain strode out and pressed the door shut behind him. I expected her to ask us questions next: who we were, why we'd come to her. She didn't. Instead, she brushed her hands against her black hem, and it seemed to me as if her fingers sank into the fabric (in the dim light it was impossible to be sure of anything). Then she bent over Alina, to study what ailed our sister.

"She has a condition," Celestia said in a gentle voice barely audible over the crackling of the embers and the hiss of boiling water. We knew how to tell the litany without prompting for every single one of the doctors who had visited Alina, all asking the exact same questions.

"Condition, they call it?" The witch glared at Celestia from under her bushy, gray-brown eyebrows. The whiteness over her eyes ran thicker. "Me can see that much with me own eyes."

I expected Celestia to argue, Elise to cry a protest. But neither of them said a word. Merile and her rats remained by the fire, unfazed, unmoving. Were they that cold, or under some sort of spell? I think the latter, but I won't ever know for sure. And now that I think of it, Scribs, it's better that way.

The witch, still bent over Alina, parted my sister's lips, and sniffed at her breath. Her bulbous nostrils flared. She shook her head. "Sweet. Why?"

I glanced at Celestia and Elise. They'd been as much as told to remain silent. Was I supposed to speak? Perhaps I was.

"She hates honey," I said. But since that alone sounded dumb, I added, "We thought she might wake up."

"Now you think?" The witch cackled. Not one of us joined the laughter. She paid no heed to us. Instead, she placed her ear against Alina's chest. She listened for a long time; such a long time that I was about to ask if there was truly something very terribly wrong with Alina.

The witch held up her bony forefinger. Her nail curled like a rusting scythe. I dared not to even breathe.

At last, the witch raised her head. Her gaze, when she unleashed it upon my sisters and me, was white and filled with wisdom beyond even her years. "Little one be with shadows."

A shiver crawled down my back. Alina spoke of shadows all the time. But that was because of the illness that affected her mind. That was what the doctors had said, at least. It's of course preposterous to think that the men of modern medicine might have been wrong. But as I huddled next to my sisters in the witch's cottage, it seemed very much possible that even though Alina is the youngest, she could somehow see and even visit the world beyond this one, the place where shadows dwell.

The witch cocked her head, waiting for us to tell her more about the shadows. I knew Celestia wouldn't—she's too rational to acknowledge this possibility. Elise wouldn't either—she thinks with her heart and would never say anything that might show our sister in a bad light. I knew, I don't know how and why, that the witch wouldn't help Alina if she sensed that we were hiding something from her. It was up to me to say it.

"A shadow of a swan visited our sister."

The witch placed her palms against the table and leaned over Alina's still body, toward us. "Swan shadow, you say?"

Scribs, I feared it then, that I'd said the wrong thing, revealed too much. The way Captain Janlav had studied the witch's cottage was a clear warning. We shouldn't tell her who we are. That might put her in danger.

"And news? This swan bear news?"

How could she possibly know? I shuddered as I thought of it, the cry from our little sister's lips. The words I wanted to be a product of her shaken mind, not the truth.

"Our honored mother is dead," Celestia said, not in a whisper as I would have done if I'd ever found the courage, but as a statement that couldn't be proven false.

The witch circled around the table, running her finger along the smooth line of our little sister's shadow. She halted before Celestia, Elise, and me, ignoring Merile. It struck me then that the witch considered Merile a child, too young to participate in the conversation meant only for adults. But in her blind eyes, I, who had yet to debut, was old enough to agree or disagree with her.

"You five . . ." This close, the witch's clothes seemed even stranger, almost translucent. She wore a dozen, no dozens of layers of thin black cloth, wrapped around her in an intricate, shifting pattern. "You come with guards."

I couldn't stand her scrutiny. As curiosity toward a witch can never end well, I glued my gaze on the floor. But that turned out to be the exact wrong thing to do, for her shadow led a life of its own. She was old and young at the same time, dancing and stooping, and I'm not kidding at all here, Scribs!

"Swan shadow deliver you news..." The witch's croaky voice trailed off. She didn't need to say more. She knew who we are.

Scribs, now that I think of it further, I shouldn't have said what I did. But the witch was the first person apart from the guards that we'd talked to since we had to leave home. The words kind of slipped out of my mouth unbidden. "Will you help us?"

Elise grabbed my arm, fingers squeezing through my blanket and sleeve. That was my chastisement. I'd confirmed to the witch she'd guessed right. And by doing so I'd placed her in some degree of danger.

"Me witch," the witch said, in what I assumed was a proud tone. "Me help little one. That be in my power. Anything else..." She rubbed her elbow against her side and made a sound that resembled a fart! But if for a moment I was flabbergasted, even amused, her next words brought me back to the world of gloom. "Fail it be."

What harsh words, even from a witch! Elise's hand remained curled around my arm, no longer a source of punishment, but one of comfort. I think the feeling was mutual.

"We accept your terms," Celestia said, and promptly proceeded to spit in her palm. Elise and I stared at her in awe. Our eldest sister was ready to make a deal with a witch! Those never came without a price, something you thought you were willing to give up, but that would cost you more than you realized.

The witch spat in her own, callused palm. She clasped hands with Celestia. She stared at her feet, at the swelling shadow around my sister. "You know what me want."

"I shall give it to you gladly," Celestia replied.

After the deal was signed, the witch set to work. She hovered around the cottage, reaching up for the ingredients she'd need in her spell. In the dimness it was hard to see, and I'd never been that good at naming plants, not unless they grew in abundance in the Summer Palace's gardens. But I did recognize birch leaves shriveled to gray-green, and fir and juniper branches. Nettles. Daffodils. And dozens, if not hundreds of plants I had no idea about, a variety of moss and lichen too. Feathers of all sorts, those of magpie set separately, those of other birds bundled together. I might have been imagining it, but amidst the plants and feathers hung bones, dried feet of chicken and rodents perhaps. Things better not to think about or risk losing sleep over.

"Summer memory, grass, bare feet." The witch lowered a long strand of what I hoped was just ordinary grass on the table, next to Alina. She glanced at Merile's unmoving shape before the fireplace and said, "Lupine stem, you see too much."

The rats by Merile's side stirred then. The black one turned to stare at the witch. So did the brown one. The witch shook her head at them. "You. No time yet. You sleep."

The rats lay down. They understood the witch's words better than I did.

I wrapped my arms across my chest. Elise noticed my discomfort. She placed her arm around my shoulder. "She's helping us."

I knew that much, but still, any sensible person is afraid of a witch. Hence, I waited till the witch had drifted to the alcove before I whispered in as low voice as I could, "But she knows too much of us."

"Hush," Elise whispered back at me. "She can do us no harm."

But the only light in the cottage came from the red-black embers. The tiny, thick windows didn't let in the Moon's light. That must have contributed to Captain Janlav's agreeing to wait outside. Our father couldn't see us. He couldn't come to our aid.

The witch returned to the table. In her right hand she clutched a clay jar. In her left a piece of dry rye bread balanced on top of a carved cup. "Sweet, one love, other hate. Give away. Again. More."

Elise's arm, still around my shoulders, tensed. The honey was meant to represent me. The rye bread? That symbolized Elise, but why and how? And why did my sister react as she did?

"One more," the witch said, motioning Celestia to meet her at the end of the table.

In the dim, red light, my fair sister resembled a spark itself. Something that strived, for a moment, with unfathomable beauty and vibrancy, but perished when it strayed too far from home, into the merciless night. "What shall it be?"

"Your finger," the witch said, and I did gasp and Elise gasped too.

But Celestia boldly held out her little finger. If she feared that the witch might cut it off, no trace of that showed on her face, or in her posture for that matter. The witch cackled as she brought her thumbnail against my sister's fingertip and promptly nicked the skin. "In cup it go."

Celestia poised her hand above the cup. A tiny red drop swelled on the curve of her fingertip. It swelled larger, burst. Her blood trickled into the cup.

"Enough," the witch said, and Celestia stepped aside, sucking her finger. Scribs, the scriptures say that our blood contains power. Then again, your pages say many things. One day I'll figure out what's nonsense and what's actually useful. I swear to you that, and if you really want to call yourself my friend one day, you'll hold me accountable for it.

"You watch," the witch said to Celestia, Elise, and me before she gestured at Merile. Our sister hadn't shifted an inch since entering the cottage. "Or you not. If you watch, you not stop. If you not watch, you not see."

Celestia nodded regally. As she's the eldest, it's her duty to watch over us. Elise shook her head and withdrew her arm from around me. She wanted no part in the witchcraft to come. I hesitated, I admit. A part of me wanted to wait by the fireplace, to warm up, to forget. But a greater part of me wanted to know what would come to pass, even if this would cost me dearly later. I shuffled to Celestia even as Elise joined Merile.

The witch grinned at me, somehow pleased by my choice. "You watch. No more. No matter what come pass."

I gripped Celestia's hand before I realized what I was doing, and forced myself to loosen my hold. She laced her fingers between mine. Our hands were so very cold, even as they had company.

The witch picked up the cup with both hands and stirred the contents. She brought it up to her blue-tinted lips and exhaled from between her crooked teeth. The exhale lasted for a long time—not as if it came from the bottom of her lungs, but from the bottom of her soles. No, not even from her soles, but from under the creaking floorboards, from the very soil of the empire.

She lowered the cup to the same level as her heart. A thin wisp of golden mist coiled up from the cup. The cottage filled with the faintest scent of summer, mixed with moments before rain, blending with that of honey pastries and backstreet alleys, and then sharpening to a piercing moment of . . . betrayal. I don't know why I thought of all these things, but I know I wasn't mistaken.

I shuffled even closer to Celestia, farther away from the witch.

The witch circled the table once more, chanting under her breath. The tone was low, barely more than a growl. But I felt it vibrate under my feet. With each round the witch made, the trembling intensified. Once she started the fifth round, I glanced up, expecting to see the dried herbs and leaves rain upon us. But not a leaf shifted.

Celestia kissed the side of my head. We shouldn't say a word, lest the spell might break. Both of us cared too deeply for Alina to risk that, and so we stood there, the thundering of our hearts the only sound we made.

The witch lowered the cup at Alina's feet. She formed a cup of flesh with her palms and waited till the golden mist filled it to the brim. When she drifted to offer it to our sister, it seemed to me her feet no longer touched the floor.

"Part lips," the witch whispered. "Taste now."

And as ordered, Alina's lips parted. She breathed through her mouth, inhaling the golden mist.

"Follow trail back to we."

Alina's body tensed, from the tip of her toes to the top of her head—clearly she was going to have another spasming attack! If Celestia hadn't held on to my arm tight, I would have rushed to Alina. I had to remind myself that I'd chosen to watch. I could have chosen not to. It was too late to regret my choice. Perhaps that was a lesson of sorts to me.

"Come back," the witch repeated.

Alina's spine arched so steeply that a cat could have leaped between her and the table. The witch brought her hand against my sister's heart and gently pushed her down. My sister didn't remain still for long. Her feet and head lifted up, up till she bent like the letter *U*.

"Come back to sisters. Come back to world."

With these words, Alina went limp. Then a shudder ran through the whole length of her body. Another one. Four of them altogether. She went limp again. The witch smiled.

"Open eyes."

I held my breath, and so did Celestia. For a moment, nothing whatsoever happened, and I feared the witch had failed, that her magic had hurt our sister, that she was lost permanently in the world beyond this one.

Alina's eyes flung open. She blinked rapidly, and then she swung up to sit on the table so that she faced Celestia and me. She said, "My eyes are open. They've been that way all the time."

I rushed to her then, and so did Celestia. We embraced her together, not quite sure how to place our arms. A moment later, Elise and Merile joined the embrace. We held her, each other, kissing temples and foreheads, rejoicing at being five again, being together.

"It be done."

The witch's croak broke us apart. We shuffled on both sides

of Alina, so that she could make her way to our sister. I didn't exactly want to move farther away from her, but you couldn't very well oppose a witch's will. No matter how seeing her might frighten my sister.

But instead, Alina stared at the witch in childlike fascination. "You are cloaked in shadows."

The witch grinned at her, offering a steaming cup. Whether it was the same she'd used before or a different one, I don't know. To be honest, I don't even want to guess.

Alina accepted the cup, but suspicion narrowed her deepset eyes.

"Drink it," the witch said. "No trick hide honey."

Alina still hesitated. She tasted just a little. A timid smile spread across her face, and it warmed my heart to such degree I couldn't even remember how it felt to be cold. "Tastes like summer."

It was then that the guards grew impatient. Captain Janlav—for who else would dare—knocked on the door. The knob turned, but the door wouldn't budge.

"Men. Always in haste." The witch glared sideways at the door. To us she said, "Stop feeding little one potions. No shadow ever harm me."

The door rattled as if a thunder were about to roll in. The witch tossed a loose end of her shawl over her shoulder. It was then that I realized it wasn't made of fabric, but a shadow of a cat. Scribs, you must believe me, this is what I saw with my very own eyes.

The door flung open, and Captain Janlav stumbled in. Noticing that we all were by the table, that we couldn't have possibly unlocked the door for him, he muttered, "So it *was* only stuck."

Then he noticed Alina, sitting on the table's edge, dangling her feet in the air. His gaze brightened and his foul mood practically leaked out of his body. "The little one is up?"

Alina set the cup down next to her. She smiled at Captain Janlav as if he were our brother, not a soldier overseeing our imprisonment. Captain Janlav strode to her and tousled her gray-brown hair. He was so glad to see her well that he didn't notice the whispered conversation that occurred between Celestia and the witch.

Scribs, again, I wasn't eavesdropping, but this is what they said to each other.

"You." The witch grabbed Celestia's arm. She pressed a small leather pouch into her hand. "Unwanted it be now. But later may be none."

"A deal is a deal," Celestia replied, pursing her hand against the witch's. "Regardless of the cost."

And Scribs, that was it. Celestia's end of the bargain.

Coldness entered the cottage in the shape of a snowy gust. The guards peered in, one after another, but didn't dare to enter. Captain Janlav must have told them to wait outside.

"We should return to the train now," Captain Janlav said. He must have been afraid of the witch, to a degree at least, for he avoided addressing her.

I wanted to protest and say that we really could stay longer, but I didn't. We had to act smart. The witch couldn't help us. She'd said as much. Now that Alina was well, we should obey the guards meekly, so that when the time came to put Celestia's plan into action, they wouldn't see it coming.

"Piggyback?" Alina asked, of all things!

Captain Janlav actually laughed. Elise swayed, as if this one sound had been a key to a lock that she'd thought forever rusted shut. He turned his back to our little sister and said, "Hop on then."

He didn't need to urge my sisters and me out. Celestia went first, because she's the eldest. I followed Elise. Merile came after me with her rats. Not one of us glanced back. Not even me, though I was tempted. Beard held the rear, seemingly relieved that we hadn't attempted to flee. The witch didn't call after us, didn't dash out of her cottage at the last moment, nothing like that. Why would she have?

We retraced our footprints to the train. I don't know how much time we'd spent in the witch's cottage, but the blue moment had come to an end and the world had turned black and white. Though I kept glancing up, I couldn't see even a trace of the Moon. But then, just as we were about to board the train, I caught the thinnest sliver of brightness, and from this I knew that our father hadn't abandoned us, but was looking after us from the sky.

Captain Janlav led us through the day carriage into our cabins. The rest of the guards remained out, to smoke their last cigarettes, I guess. My sisters and I kissed Alina good night, not exactly eager to part from her.

"I'm fine," she said, time after time. She even giggled. Whatever magic the witch had unleashed on her seemed to work better than any of Nurse Nookes's potions.

We retreated into our cabins. Captain Janlav locked the doors. I lay on my bed for a long time, fully dressed, absolutely sure I could never fall asleep. After a while, the train lurched into motion. It must have taken some time and effort to reheat the engine. I closed my eyes for a moment, only to wake up come morning.

A timid knock announced the arrival of the silent servant.

I felt tempted to ignore it, but that would have meant missing the opportunity to wash. I quickly got up and smoothed my skirts. There was no smoothing my hair from the tangled braids—incidents of this sort are what separate me from Elise.

"Come in," I said.

The guard accompanying the servant unlocked the door. The servant offered me a pitcher of lukewarm water through the barely wide enough crack. I accepted it with whatever gratitude I could muster up.

I washed my face and hands sluggishly. Risking Merile's snarky remarks, I decided not to wash further. The morning was too chilly for me to care to undress.

I sat down on my bed to wait for the guards to escort us to the day carriage. I reached for the nightstand's drawer to retrieve you, Scribs. Then I remembered that I'd left you in the day carriage, stashed under the divan's pillow. I imagined in horror what would happen if the servant or guards had happened upon you. One thought only eased my mind. This particular silent servant isn't keen on cleaning.

Another knock came from the door. I bounced up, eager to retrieve you, Scribs.

When I exited my cabin, Captain Janlav had already roused Elise. He waited by Celestia's door, the one closest to the day carriage. Merile appeared soon after, with her rats. Even Alina made it out of her cabin before Celestia. Boy ushered her up the corridor, toward us. She ran, squealing.

"What's taking Celestia this long," Merile said aloud, the very thing that I, too, wondered.

I thought of the witch then, of the deal she'd struck with Celestia. What if Captain Janlav were to open the door, only to find our eldest sister missing? The Moon bless me for thinking of this even in passing, but what if her plan was to escape alone? No doubt she'd send someone to rescue us later. I'm almost sure of that.

"Celestia," Captain Janlav called through her cabin's door. When he received no reply, he cupped his palm against his ear and held it against the panel. "Everyone is waiting for you."

He tapped his right foot a good ten times. A flicker of suspicion crossed his face as he retreated a step and very unceremoniously pulled open the door.

I couldn't take it anymore then, and neither could Elise. We darted after him, into the cabin. Oh, Scribs, it was horrible and horribly embarrassing!

Celestia lay on her bed, wrapped in a stained sheet. A most terrifying case of wretched days must have crept upon her during the night. For she'd bled all over the sheet and the mattress and her dress. Sometimes I get feverish during mine and suffer from cramps. But my sister's face . . . color had fled her cheeks, and a cold sheen of sweat clung to her forehead.

"By the wretched days," I muttered under my breath for the benefit of Captain Janlav, for he couldn't possibly fathom the extent of the bloody horror that women faced monthly.

"Uh-oh . . ." Captain Janlav actually blushed and stepped aside to let Elise and me pass. He moved to block the entrance. The Moon bless him for that.

"Close the door, will you?" Elise snapped, kneeling before Celestia. Our sister's embarrassment needed no further witnesses. "And ask the servant to bring water and towels."

I didn't quite know what to do. Luckily, Elise was in much better control of herself. She checked Celestia's forehead for temperature. "Can you hear us, Celestia?"

Celestia turned on her side to face us. She muttered something under her breath, still half sleepy or dazed by pain. "Elise? Sibilia? What are you doing here?"

I was too flustered to reply, and so I stared at her stained sheets. Celestia followed my gaze. But rather than looking shocked or even abashed, a faint smile spread across her face. "I have paid the price. Everything is well now."

What she meant by that, I can't even begin to guess, Scribs.

While I was still puzzled by Celestia's words, Elise helped our sister up, to sit on the bed's edge. The exhausted glance Elise cast at me revealed that the dread that turned me sluggish had also crossed her mind. First Alina. Now Celestia.

The servant brought cold water and towels. Elise and I assisted Celestia in cleaning as much as she'd let us. We turned aside as she used the chamber pot, but when she pushed it under the bed, I noticed that she bled very heavily. Was this the witch's doing, somehow? Or has my sister always suffered from really, really bad wretched days?

"Let us not keep them waiting," Celestia said once she was fully dressed and padded up. She leaned against the wall as another set of cramps tore through her body—that much was obvious from her grimace.

"Shouldn't you rest here for the day?" I asked. Elise nodded, echoing my opinion. "They really can't be as cruel as to deny you that."

Celestia met us with that celestial gaze of hers, blue as the skies, deep as the oceans. "And break the routine? Don't be silly, my dear sisters."

With that said, she swayed to the door and announced us ready. Our younger sisters had already been escorted to the day carriage. Captain Janlav led us there to join them.

Though Celestia insisted she would be fine resting on her

customary sofa chair, I urged Captain Janlav to help her to my divan. As soon as she lay down, she dozed off. We had to practically chase the captain away. And he didn't stay that way for long—he kept on checking on us every half hour.

Scribs, I have a theory that I'll tell you only under one condition. You mustn't call me silly or laugh at me. You mustn't claim me superstitious.

I believe Captain Janlav's fate is permanently interwoven with ours. Even if the anxiety he first felt for Alina's well-being and now for Celestia's is that which he feels for his own, there is more to him. Kindness that shouldn't exist in a soldier that the gagargi has chosen as his pawn.

Ugh. I don't want to think of the gagargi and his plans now. I will stop writing after this paragraph, lest I might run out of ink. Soon, there should be lunch. I hope against all hope that there will be dessert. Even a morsel of cinnamon biscuit would do wonders to my spirit. It's been a miserable two days, and at some point next week, I'll need to face the wretched days of my own, and I'm not looking forward to them. At. All.

Chapter 9

Elise

The train squeals akin to a child of iron whose limbs are torn apart, like a daughter of ice about to receive a shattering blow, like a shadow of a maiden abandoned into a lightless cave, like a glorious figurehead crafted from silver that the journey will tarnish and that can never quite be polished back to her former shine.

I stir from the shallow sleep, the only kind of sleep I have known for weeks, as I bump against the cabin's wall. I remain there, leaning against the lacquered panel that seeps coldness through my clothes onto my skin, then onward into my bones. This isn't the first time the train screams nor the first it halts in the middle of the night.

Yet something is different, the stillness and slowness of time. I quickly get up, slip my feet into the sabots that have long since ceased to chafe me. Though the curtains of my cabin are drawn down, though the guards have told us not to look out, I swiftly part them.

We are in the middle of nowhere, where the vast expanse of snow stretches on forever, glittering regardless of the cost that such display of wealth might require. The sky is black and scattered with stars. My father's gaze is kind, a golden halo against the velvet.

I know at once, this isn't a planned stop.

For a moment, my heart throbs and my breathing comes in dizzying gasps. My fingers tremble as I slip out of my nightgown, into the simple woolen dress. Even though the buttons are big and on the front, I struggle to fasten them. If Lily were here, she'd hum one of her melancholy tunes. But she's not, and I don't know what became of my friend. She never revealed to me what her plan would be once the side we both supported triumphed. I thought her cautious, not wary of me, but perhaps I was wrong about that, too. Perhaps it's better I don't know what became of her, just as she's blessed not to know what has and will eventually happen to me.

I lift my mattress's edge and retrieve the stash of sequin necklaces. Celestia has a plan, but she hasn't entrusted me with the details either. I loop the thin chains around my neck, around my wrists. This might be the night we are at last rescued, and in case it is, I want to be ready for every eventuality. For I'm partially at fault in my family's demise.

I thought I could cease to be a Daughter of the Moon. I funded the insurgence. I gave away jewelry a thousand times more valuable than the sequins that pinch the back of my neck, that grow cool even as they press against my skin. Back when life was simpler, when we still lived in the palace and I sneaked out with the man who no longer remembers my name, I cherished the thought of absolute independence. I wanted to be a woman amongst others, nothing more. I naively thought the revolution would set me free. It didn't.

I thought that I was so smart. I foresaw an exile of an undetermined length, not this bone-rattling journey to a destination yet unnamed. I knew to expect a wave of uncertainty, one that would pass soon after the people had accepted the new order. I thought my sisters and I could then return without our titles, to live a normal life. How foolish was I in my dreams!

Wait, are those approaching steps? I shuffle to the door and press my ear against the panel. Someone is running down the length of the corridor beyond. No doubt it's the guard on the night watch. I don't know if he's the one who now ignores me, or one of the others that go by the nicknames my younger sisters have bestowed on them: Beard, Boy, Belly, Boots, and Tabard. While the nightly isolation is a source of comfort to me, for it gives me time to reflect, the thought that they may enter and leave as they please unsettles me. As it must unsettle both Celestia and Sibilia, though we never talk about it—how could we, without causing more distress to our younger sisters? Even though our guards rather pretend we don't exist, isn't it just a matter of time before someone less civil boards the train, someone who thinks that a captured Daughter of the Moon doesn't need to be revered, but should instead be tarnished?

The train has fallen silent. I squeeze my ear against the panel so hard that it hurts. I can distinguish but faint cursing. For a long while, there's nothing else. My sisters and I never make sounds during the nights. This is something Celestia forbade, and upon her insistence, we stick to the routine. She has a plan. She has thought through every eventuality, even the ones that the rest of us are too frightened to consider. That is how she is, rational beyond reason.

Even the cursing ceases. I pace the short length of my cabin. Five steps to the window. Five steps back to the door. Perhaps it was nothing. The train could have halted for many different reasons. Perhaps it hit a snow bank. Perhaps the coal shoveler fell asleep. Perhaps . . .

Then I hear it. Someone strides up the corridor. The rhythm, the footfall of hard heels, reveals haste. Could it be our potential rescuer, one of our seeds or a nobleman loyal to my family, Count Albusov or Marques Frususka, leading a platoon of soldiers in blue? Or is it someone who wishes us ill? How can I find out for sure?

I grab the gray blanket from my bed, but for a few surging heartbeats, I hesitate to pound the door. Why? For no good reason other than fear.

I bring the bottom of my right fist against the panel. Again. And again. If this is a rescue, there's nothing to be ashamed of, apart from my disheveled state. If it's one of the guards, I will have to come up with a very good excuse indeed.

The steps stagger to a halt before my door.

"In here!" I shout hoarsely, not daring to be too loud. For if it's neither our rescuer nor one of the guards . . .

A lot is at stake here; not only what will become of me but also the well-being of my sisters. My throat tightens as I think of them. Are they sleeping through these moments? Or are they lying awake in their beds, too afraid to say a word? Do they think they are dreaming? Do they think this a nightmare?

A key turns in the lock. Would our rescuer have the key? How about those who despise us? Only one way to find out.

I push the door open, only to come face-to-face with the man whom I once loved.

"Yes?" His puzzled gaze seems darker than I remember, his moustache thicker, and his stubble has grown into a beard that covers his strong jaw and creeps up his cheeks.

No rescue then. No ill will either. Yet my heart sags, sinks into the bottom of the sea like a weighted sack. One excuse is as good as any, some more believable than others. At least the squeal in my voice is genuine. "What was the ruckus about? Why have we halted?"

He leans on the wall, his left hand resting looped against his blue winter coat's leather belt. His gloves are red. A dusting of snow covers his shoulders. The strap of his rifle runs across his chest. When he speaks, his tone of voice is perfectly polite and formal. "We hit a frozen snow bank. It's being cleared now."

So that was it. I should be more disappointed. But for some reason I'm not. This is the first time we have spoken in private since the night we boarded the train, over four weeks ago. That night was the first I noticed the change in how he acted toward me. Was it from the shame of turning against my family? No, that's not why it happened.

"You should go back to bed," Captain Janlav says. Once I named him the captain of my heart. Now I can't bring myself to address him by anything other than the rank he gained in my mother's service. Curious thought, is he still entitled to that?

He shifts to push the door closed. I brace myself against it. "No."

I do this because . . . Because I don't want him to go. Because I want to see if anything remains of the man whose heart I once thought I knew inside out.

"No?" His mellow voice bears a hint of amusement. He still seems to revere my sisters and me. The other guards and servants treat us more like prisoners. It's him who talks with us when the rest resort to silence.

"Please let me out, even if it's only for a moment." The pleading tone is genuine, and I hate myself for that. But it's been over a week since we visited the witch, and though since then they have let us out at some of the smaller towns, it's been only for enough time to stretch our legs. Celestia calls that a victory. No doubt her plan depends on these excursions growing longer and more frequent.

Captain Janlav shakes his head curtly. He still keeps his hair in a topknot, but he no longer shaves the sides of his head. One day he will sport an auburn mane much like a lion's. Just as I'm changing, so is he. But whether he's becoming a dangerous man or just a different man, that I can't yet say. "So that when I'd look aside, you could wander off on your own. No, I don't think so."

I roll my eyes at him, a gesture better suited to Merile or dear Sibs. He makes it sound as if he's concerned that I'd fall off a cliff or be captured by someone else. Then let's play by his rules. "We are in the middle of nowhere. There's no one around for miles. My father's gaze is bright. No one can harm me tonight."

His brows rise.

"I peeked through the window."

He chuckles. "Now did you?"

"I did."

He studies me for a while, the uncombed hair that falls tangled on my shoulders, the blanket I clutch against my chest. I know he finds me beautiful, though he no longer says it aloud. He gazes at me for so long that I'm sure he has noticed the looped necklace or bracelets that the thick fabric of my dress barely conceal, that he will push the door closed and lock it behind him. But at last, he says, "Come, then, but be forewarned, it's freezing outside."

Before he can change his mind, I hasten out of the cabin. When we were allotted our cabins, it was done in the order of age. Celestia's cabin is closest to the day carriage, at the end of the corridor, to my left. As I walk toward the other end of the carriage, I pass Sib's, Merile's, and Alina's cabins. I hear nothing that would indicate that any of them are awake. That guarantees nothing. Celestia suspects that Alina doesn't sleep at nights. My little sister has lately talked more and more of the shadows, though as the youngest it's not possible for her to glimpse into the world beyond this one. I suspect the decay that affects her mind has spread during this journey. I know for sure that we have run out of her medicine.

It's horrifying to come to the conclusion that there's nothing you can do for your sister. And since this is the case, and since this is one of the rare chances to breathe uncaptured air, I stride past little Alina's cabin.

When we come to the heavy door that leads out of the train, Captain Janlav pulls a key ring from his belt. The dozen keys of brass and iron jingle with promises of freedom. He turns his back to me so that I can't see which one he uses to open the door. It pains me that he doesn't trust me. But if I were in his boots, would I trust me either?

Come to think of it, I did trust him with everything. That didn't end too well for me or my sisters. Or our mother . . . Even if we have only Alina's word of her demise, Celestia believes it true. Our mother is dead. Eventually, my sister will become the next empress.

Unless something were to happen to her. And something might well happen now that the battle lines have been drawn and the soldiers' hands are bloody on both sides. A betrayal or murder most vile, poison slipped in tea or a knife thrust between the lowest ribs.

The door squeals as Captain Janlav pushes it open, an interruption most welcome. Immediately the winter exhales a snowy breath upon us. He glances at me, grinning. "Do you still want to go out?"

I wrap the gray blanket better around my shoulders and brush past him onto the covered platform, fleeing the ghastly thoughts. He closes the door behind us, but doesn't lock it. Why would he? Where else would I return than back inside?

The night is very black. The rails stretch before us, the two lines of iron reaching toward each other, but never quite meeting. I used to think of the railroads as the veins of my mother's empire. Now, looking at the grimness of iron against snow, I think of them as wounds that won't ever heal.

A chiming click of metal breaches the silence. I turn to see Captain Janlav flicking open a silver cigarette case. It's the one I gave him as a gift, before he told me of the cause, of the life beyond the palace walls. How curious for him to have kept it when all of us lead equally austere lives here on this train. Why didn't he donate it to fund the cause?

"What?" He glances at me from under his brows before his attention drifts back to the cigarettes and the case itself, the delicate crescent clasp and the etched, straight lines representing rays of the Moon, master workmanship at its finest.

"It's a beautiful case you have. How did you come by it?" Does he really remember nothing?

He shrugs as he lifts a cigarette to his lips. His moustache is unoiled. Whiskers curl against the rolled paper. "I really can't say. Curious, though, isn't it?"

I wrap the blanket tighter around myself. The chains of sequins weigh heavy against the vulnerable skin of my neck. He really, really doesn't remember the moments we once cherished. That is a relief to me. There was a time I thought he had knowingly deceived me, that he had only acted to get into my favor, that the love we had shared hadn't been true. It was only after Celestia told me of what Gagargi Prataslav had done to her that I understood he must have altered Captain Janlav, too.

As Captain Janlav blows smoky clouds into the night, I feel not only cold but also dizzy. I seek support from the rail, lean on my left hand. The metal bites my flesh with teeth of ice. My whole body jolts, yet I curl my fingers around the rail. I'm past caring about pain. Every single one of us was led astray, in one way or the other.

Celestia feared for the empire's future and consulted Gagargi Prataslav for advice. He stole a part of her soul and used her as a puppet to advance his wayward plans. He . . . it's too terrible to think of, but I owe my sister not to ignore it, not to pretend that what befell her could really be forgotten and hence hadn't happened at all. The gagargi manipulated his way into her bed. He sowed his seed, and made her think she wanted it.

"Watch out or your fingers will freeze and you'll never get them off that bar." The voice belongs to the one who doesn't remember who I became, only who I was before we first met. He touches my left hand, and even if I wanted to, I can't move an inch. "Ah, too late."

I stand so very still as he attempts to pry my fingers loose. To no avail. The metal pinches my skin possessively. I'm stuck to the rail. How embarrassing.

"May I?" he asks, bending his head close to my hand. What is he after? What have I got to lose?

"You may."

He blows gently at my hand, moist clouds of salvation. On the third breath, I manage to free my hand. My fingertips, the inside of my palm, are raw red. My handprint remains on the rail, a dull, dark shape against the faint sheen of ice.

He moves as if to examine my hand, a crease of alarm on his forehead. I quickly hide my hand under the blanket, against my palpitating heart. "I'm not hurt."

But Celestia was, still is. My sister confided in me when she didn't bleed when she should have. I assured her that it was due to stress only. That happens often enough, I have heard. She didn't say it out loud, and it would have been too early to know still, but she feared that the gagargi's seed had taken root inside her.

The deal my sister made with the witch benefitted them both. But when trading with witches, the cost always runs deeper than one can anticipate. Even a week after swallowing the potion, Celestia continues to bleed. No longer as heavily, but . . . She must fear that the witch's potion has left a permanent mark on her body, that . . . No, I won't think of it. Our mother is dead. Celestia will be the empress, even if there hasn't been and won't be a ceremony in the near future, even if she hasn't yet married the Moon. Her daughters, let there be many of them, will rule after her. Not mine.

"We should go back inside," Captain Janlav says.

He's right. My left hand aches. The fingertips hurt as though a heavy object had fallen on them. And yet . . . If the cost of freedom, even a momentary one, is pain, I would be a fool to not pay it.

"Not yet," I reply, and without waiting for his answer, I climb down the steep, narrow ladder, onto the snow-veiled tracks.

His boots crunch against the snow as he jumps after me. He reaches out to grab my shoulder. I evade him. I stride farther away from the train. Perhaps I can't flee, and I won't, not without my sisters. But maintaining the illusion of freedom, for even a moment, is worth more than anything I have ever owned.

"Please . . ." The pain in his voice, it pierces my heart like a spear. "Please don't try to run away from me. I'm only trying to keep you safe."

I falter to a halt, for the crossties between the rails are slippery. I hear him stop behind me, the uneasy rhythm of his breath. The walls of snow around us are stained by coal smoke and stripes of blue paint from the carriages. This aisle, almost a tunnel, reminds me of a time gone past, of the times I followed him through other tunnels. Curious, how much has changed and yet so little.

"I know I shouldn't say this . . ." A silvery click betrays his need for another cigarette. And then later, the wisp of malty smoke his hesitation.

"Then don't," I reply, tired of games. Though who am I to blame him—wasn't this little escapade of mine a silly move on my part? For where would I go from here, in the middle of the night? Follow the trails to the village where we stopped for fuel earlier? Why tease myself with a prospect of freedom when I know all too well that our lives are not for us to live but are in the hands of others?

"But I want to, need to say it aloud." His fingers come to rest against my shoulder, on the blanket, lightly like raindrops. He coaches me to turn around, and I can't resist his plea. And yet, he lacks the courage to meet my gaze. He stares past me, into the distance. "Sometimes I feel like I've known you for much longer than for the duration of this journey."

Just as the icy rail burned my hand earlier, his words scorch my heart and mind alike. A part of him does remember me.

This thought warms me, though by now my eyelashes must be frozen, though my earlobes feel numb, though my cheeks ache when I smile.

"Is that a happy smile or one reserved for fools?" He knows me well indeed, even if he doesn't realize it.

What do I have to lose if I tell him now? This information can't possibly endanger whatever plan Celestia has in mind. "We have known each other since last autumn, since we danced at little Alina's name day festivities."

He laughs. His chuckles form white clouds that are cold by the time they reach me. "That's impossible. I would remember that."

"You courted me for months," I say, slightly annoyed at him, at everything.

"Don't be a cruel woman." He fidgets with the cigarette, clearly tempted to toss it aside but aghast at wasting an almost untouched treat. My father decides for him—the cigarette slips from his gloved fingers. His sad sigh echoes a loss of immeasurable magnitude. "Not when I've made a fool of myself already."

Every breath hurts, but not because of the low temperature. It hurts me that he thinks me cruel, that I'm jesting at his expense. Even worse, he might think that I'm trying to manipulate him, wrap him around my little finger so that my sisters and I could at last go free.

That's of course an idea, one that I can only see failing, and besides, that isn't what I want now. I want him to believe me. I want him to remember what we shared for those few blessed months. "You took me to workhouses and hospitals."

"Stop it now." He stomps his heel on the cigarette and crushes it against the frozen crosstie. "I should have . . . I should have known better. Oh, I've heard it said that the Daughters of the Moon are witches better to watch out for. Now I see what they meant by it. Don't say a word more to me."

I want to slap him so badly. Instead I force myself to simply take hold of his hand. I'm not sure where my actions will lead me, but any place is better than letting the distance between us grow, for letting him continue believing that he never loved me. For that hurts; it hurts more than I'm capable of admitting to myself. "You took me to an orphanage where we shared bread with the nameless children. You wanted to carry me over the puddles, but I didn't let you. That would have gathered too much attention."

His eyes narrow a fraction. His hand feels tense through the red leather of his glove. "I don't recall such."

"You also took me to a workhouse where sounds harsh and loud filled the night. The very air smelled of sticky tar and dry hemp. There, the poor worked in the smoke of the cheapest tallow candles. They squinted at the lengths of rope, fraying it to pick oakum. To me, they all looked the same. At first, I didn't realize why. I wondered, was it the desperation writ all over their faces? The concentration of one desperate enough to give his life into the hands of others in exchange for something, anything to eat? But no, in the end I realized it was their faded gray uniforms, so worn that no two garments looked exactly the same, so valued that every single person in the room wore theirs with something that eerily resembled pride."

"Please don't." Captain Janlav runs his free hand through his hair, scattering snowflakes. He lives in denial or then simply doesn't remember, but he wonders. How could I possibly know these details? No one would tell such to a Daughter of the Moon. No one would write these ugly truths on paper, not even as their reflections about the scriptures. "I'm just a man, and I'm not sure of many things, but I'm sure that before I was tasked with the honor of escorting you and your sisters to safety, I had never seen you, only heard of you." He winces as though struck by a sudden headache. "And even if I had, I would never have taken a girl like you to a workhouse."

Can the gagargi's spell be somehow undone? I glance up at the Moon. My father gazes back at me kindly. He helped Celestia to break the spell the gagargi had cast on her. Will he help me?

"You took me to a hospital," I say, silently praying for my father to come to my aid. "We saw the halls crammed with beds. We walked through the long corridors. We heard the involuntary whimpers, the escaped sobs and sniffs. We greeted the men who had once been so proud, who had marched to war in their prime. They were that no more, but forgotten; out of sight, out of mind."

"Stop it." He tugs his hand—once, twice—as if yearning to be released. But I can't let go of him now, can't heed his plea. I can remember everything as if it had happened mere heartbeats earlier, not in another time and age.

"You led me down the aisle into a vast, white hall. There lay the ones who suffered the most. The fathers and sons, the uncles and cousins, every single one equal in their pain. Men that had faced cannons, who now missed a leg or an arm. Or more. Men with bandages wrapped around their heads, over their unseeing eyes and unhearing ears. Men with wounds that . . . stank of rot, their bandages dirty, unchanged. You took me to the very men who went to war because my mother so demanded, the very men she forgot once they were no longer of use to her."

"No!" He yanks his hand back with such force that I lose him. I have gone too far, or perhaps then not far enough. And yet, I don't dare to touch him again. What if he was even partially right? What if my father or even I do indeed possess a power to make people act as benefits us? If I were to take further advantage of that . . . I would be no better than the gagargi.

I wait patiently, dreading that he will never speak to me again. I don't know how long we have been out already. I don't know when the train will depart. Perhaps soon. But I can't hurry him, not now, even though this may be the only opportunity we have for this conversation.

"You can't know this." His voice is hoarse, that of a frightened boy. "You can't. How could you? You've lived a sheltered life of leisure, in the halls and hallways of the finest palaces. How could you have ever even wanted to know the truth?"

I tilt my chin up, a gesture Celestia resorts to when argued against. How infuriatingly can a man act? How can I still care for him this much? "Because you showed it to me." He flinches, and I regret my harshness. It's not his fault he doesn't remember. I add out of remorse, "Silly."

He reaches out for me, and I'm acutely aware of the silver pressing against my skin. I shift minutely, so that his fingers come to rest against my shoulder, not my neck. I meet his eyes with a questioning gaze. His eyes are the same as before, the brown of young pines. And yet, the gaze is different. But I think . . . Is there a flicker of recollection there?

His lips part, and I lean toward him. Because I miss him. I miss being with him.

"No," he says, pulling his hand away. Again. "We must not. It would interfere with my duty."

I feel like laughing and crying, both at the same time. My

lips burn with the cold, not with his kiss. My voice trembles with what may be chagrin. "Your duty?"

"To see you safely to our destination." It sounds as if he were repeating a mantra, something enforced in his mind by foul means. He crosses his hands behind his back and nods toward the carriage. He wants us to return. "If you must know, it isn't exactly easy, to keep another human being contained for an extended period of time, even if it's for their own safety and to ensure the future of the Crescent Empire."

This lie . . . I want to laugh maniacally, I want to argue, but I bite my tongue. He sounds so serious, proud even. Perhaps it's not a lie to him. Perhaps that's why the other guards avoid us, so that they won't have to remember why the doors are locked and curtains drawn, why one of them has to sit in the corridor ready to spring into action while the others play cards and smoke cigarettes.

"I never assumed it would be," I reply at last. My father still gazes kindly at us. If he doesn't feel anger, neither should I.

"It's not only that," he says, chin pressed against his chest, but not to keep himself warm. Something weighs heavy on his mind. It's curious that I know him though he doesn't know me.

It strikes me then. He's a captain, the one in the lead. He has no one else to confide in than the very person he thinks he's tasked to guard. "What is it, then?"

He glances over his shoulder, at the rails—no, onward—at the plains we have crossed, into the towns we have left behind. In his eyes lives regret, longing to change a decision made or perhaps an act done in haste. "When Alina fell ill, when we halted in that town . . ."

"Yes?" I prompt, dreading the answer, every slipping step that carries us closer to the carriage and silence. The witch, no matter that she helped us, frightens me. She saw things in our shadows, shapes she wouldn't speak of, and the bargain she made with Celestia left my sister weak.

"You hate us already," Captain Janlav says. "Don't you?"

I don't say a word. So that's it, then. He has done something so despicable that he expects to be called a monster.

"You would hate us even more if you knew the lengths to which we have gone to protect you and your sisters."

"Try me," I reply more dryly than I had intended. The cold air has chafed my throat sore. I might catch my death because of this excursion, but I'm past caring about that.

"Perhaps I will." He glances at the carriage, at the door he left unlocked, as if to measure how many words he has time to say before all talk must cease. "After you'd boarded the train, we argued about it long and hard. I didn't want to do it, but what choice did we have? Even as blind as she was, what if she somehow recognized you? What if she'd tell someone? Not that she seemed the type. But what if those who wish to harm you caught her in their hands and interrogated her. People speak when they're in pain. They'll do anything to make the agony stop."

I had practically betrayed my family to escape the darkness of my own mind. What he's saying . . . As I shake my head, my blanket shifts. Cold gnaws at my throat, down my back, into my belly. "No . . ."

"I had to send Beardard back."

He doesn't need to tell me more. I can see the sad scene unfolding before my eyes. Beard wading through the snow banks, rifle swinging against his back. The small cottage at the end of the lane. The witch hearing the approaching sounds, the snow crunching under his boots. He wasn't there to ask her to remain silent, but to unsling his rifle and make sure that she would take what she had seen and heard to her grave.

At that moment, I can't imagine how I ever could have loved this ruthless man.

"The thing is," Captain Janlav says when we are but ten steps away from the carriage, "when he came to the end of the lane, to the very spot where we'd smoked a pack of cigarettes mere hours earlier, he found nothing. Nothing at all."

I glance at him from the corner of my eye. His serious gaze is riveted on the train. I can't decipher if he's lying to me in a futile attempt to soothe me. A part of me doesn't even want to try.

"Our footprints led to an abandoned yard. But there was nothing there. No trace of the old woman. No trace of the wee cottage. Not even a shadow remained."

He meets my gaze at last. His eyes gleam with . . . earnestness. Does he really believe he's serving me, not the gagargi? Does he really speak the truth?

"Beardard returned, ashen-faced. We thought he'd been drinking. Or smoking dusk. I took two good men with me and retraced our earlier path. Only to find out that Beardard hadn't been mistaken. Where I'd expected to find the witch, I found but a magpie staring accusingly at us."

As he escorts me back to the train, I decide he isn't lying, at least not consciously. But can I ever forgive this? The witch may have escaped, but that doesn't change the fact that he ordered her silenced.

When we reach the steps leading to the platform, he offers me his hand, to help me climb the steep metal steps. But I'd rather scorch my hand again than accept his help, and that's what I do. Once I'm up, I glance at him from over my shoulder.

His expression is one of utter confusion, and I do feel as if I should be the one apologizing. "I..."

But we are saved from further awkwardness by a shrill hoot that pierces the night.

He stills. His posture tenses, and his gaze glazes over. When he looks up at me, he no longer sees me, but someone else. A Daughter of the Moon. Whatever I might have been tempted to say no longer matters.

"The guards are done with the snow." He quickly climbs up after me. As if nothing had changed. And yet everything has. "Time to return inside."

I brush past him, into the confinement that has become home for my sisters and me.

Chapter 10

Celestia

I know every town and city, their names and exact coordinates.
I know every stretch of railroad, every junction and station. I
have flown from north to south, over the mountains and tundras. I know the face of the Crescent Empire, for I am the
empress-to-be.

The pearl bracelets weigh on my gown's two pockets,
through the wool, against my thighs. There are no clocks in the
carriage. I measure the passing of time by the beat of my heart
and the rhythm of the train clacking against the tracks. Today
is the day I have been waiting for patiently for five weeks and
two days.

I sip tea from the earless teacup, studying my sisters from
over the gilded brim. They know I have a plan. They know I
haven't shared it with them. It is for their own good. What they
don't know, they can't reveal. I count the clacks. The train's
speed is constant, but eventually it will slow down. When it
does so, my sisters and I will flee.

Elise combs her red-gold hair, one long stroke at a time.
She studies her reflection in the silver hand mirror, lush lips
pursed, gray eyes narrowed. I want to tell her to hurry, but it
isn't yet the time. I must remain in full control of myself. I can't
afford to act hastily.

Sibilia reads the scriptures, elbows leaning against the marble-topped table. Her hair is braided against her scalp, her fingers buried in between the strands as if she is struggling to understand the passages. I don't blame her. I know the scriptures by heart, but our father's wisdom evades me. Perhaps when I marry him, he will reveal to me the secrets no mere mortal may possess, what he has seen from the sky.

That is one of the reasons why we ended up here. It was I who failed the empire when I fell under Gagargi Prataslav's spell. If I had been wiser, it would have never happened. I think.

"Jump here, Rafa," Merile calls at her dog from her usual spot on the sofa at the other end of the carriage. "Up here."

The brown dog jumps. It lands on the sofa, tail wagging wildly. My sister laughs.

"No, here." Alina pats the cushion on the sofa opposite to Merile's. "Come back here, silly dog."

And the dog lands on the floor, and then up it goes again.

My smile is a faint crescent, one I want to cherish, one I don't want anyone else to see. My sisters, they are the future of the empire. Once I thought this role was for me to fill. Now I know that it will not be. Not for long.

If my plan works today . . . No, not if, but when. When my plan works, we will be free, but there will be a lot of work to be done, to bring my people together, to repair the damage the gagargi's plot has brought unto the empire.

"You look thoughtful," Elise says between two long strokes. The golden strands caught between the comb's spikes glimmer under the timid light of the osprey chandelier.

I lower the half-empty cup and reply, "It occurred to me that you understand well indeed this empire: what we need, what the people need."

Elise's hand pauses mid-stroke. Her head cants to the right. Her lips part as if she wanted to say something, but then changed her mind. She isn't the same girl who she was before, at the palace. The weeks in the train have changed her. "Perhaps I once thought I knew it. Now, I'm not so sure."

Mother, the Moon bless her soul, always said that a wise person is the one who can admit that they don't know everything. That is why even the empresses have advisors. But mother, oh mother, you chose your advisors poorly. You should have never let Gagargi Prataslav stay at the court, not when it became so obvious, so soon, that he could influence everyone he spoke to.

But mother is dead, and hence beyond blame. If anyone should be blamed, it is me. It was I who fell under the gagargi's spell. It was I who . . .

I have rid myself of him. I have bled myself off his seed. I am no longer under his spell. Today, I will soar across the blue skies, over the frozen lakes.

"Sibs, won't you close that terribly boring book and come and braid my hair?" Elise calls at our sister.

Sibilia stirs from her thoughts. She uncurls her fingers from her hair and tenderly presses the book of holy scriptures shut. "Sure. I need a break anyway. The thing is, I have this nagging feeling that some of the passages contain genuinely important knowledge. But I just can't figure out which ones."

"Oh, Sibs!" Elise's laughter chimes like silver bells. "I'm sure that no one aside from the gagargis can."

Sibilia bangs her knee against the table's leg as she gets up. She curses under her breath, then blushes. She is neither in full control of her body nor her mind.

"What sort of braid would you like to have?" Sibilia in-

206 • Leena Likitalo

quires once she stands behind Elise.

Elise glances at me, as if asking how much time we have left. The clacks still come regularly. I nod minutely.

"Try something new, will you?" Elise replies. Though I haven't told her that today is the day, she senses that the time has come. Soon we will fly free.

Fly. That is my swan-self's thought. No matter how I pretend, I am not in full control of myself either. The gagargi still holds a strand of my soul, what he managed to breathe in that night I shattered the bead. What I shelter in my body contains traces of the swan he killed that night.

That swan has become my companion. I have lost some of my own memories, but gained ones that aren't mine. At times I imagine I have wings and remember only when I move my arms that I will never be able to take to the air again. At times I tilt my head, only to find my neck too short. At times I think of nesting.

I lift the teacup to my lips and close my eyes. It was my own choice to swallow the witch's potion, though she warned me of the price. I will not cry. I will not fret. It was I who made the decision. No one else.

"The train is slowing speed," Sibilia says.

I realize it then, too. How long did I dwell on my thoughts, in my regrets? Elise's braid is complete, a red-gold crown circling her head. Too long.

I take a deep breath and lower the cup onto the saucer. The moment we have awaited for weeks is upon us at last. That is all that matters. "Gather around me, my sisters. Come and hear my plan."

For a moment, they just stare at me. Gray eyes, brown eyes, dark eyes. Elise quickly picks up the silver mirror and slips it inside her dress. Sibilia pockets the comb and claims the book of scriptures with the fountain pen clipped against its spine. Merile dashes to me, Alina at her heels, the dogs bouncing after them.

"Finally!" Merile gasps, beaming at me. The rest of us have paled during our confinement, but her skin still bears the hue of endless summer days. "I thought you'd never tell us."

I smile at her despite myself. She is eleven and impatient. She deserves to run through meadows with her dogs, unguarded, unrestricted. "But now I will."

My sisters listen in unwavering silence as I outline my plan to them. It is based on the routines we have established during our weeks of imprisonment. Since Alina's seizure, we have been allowed out to stretch our legs while the train is refueled and watered. There are three reasons for this: the guards think us docile now; the unrests never reached this far north; and, finally, they fear how the gagargi would react if we were to succumb to the ill health that I hinted might follow if we were kept indoors for too long. Elise has a fourth reason, one I am not quite sure I believe. She claims the guards think that they are keeping us contained for our own safety, that they are . . . protecting us. Could the gagargi really enforce such by tampering with a man's mind? If that is the case, there is even more reason for us to abandon this train today.

"I have something for each of you." I pull the pearl bracelets out from the pockets I added to my gown the night before. What once was Elise's ball gown is now our means for funding our escape. "Keep them hidden. Use them only when you must."

Elise knew of this part of my plan. There is more: the necklaces made of silver sequins. She raises her right eyebrow at me, but doesn't ask aloud. She can guess the answer. I am saving the sequins and my dress in case . . . No, we shall not fail. But a wise empress always has a contingency plan.

Alina snatches her bracelet and loops it twice around her thin wrist. She raises her hand up and admires it, beaming. "It's very pretty!"

Sibilia turns the bracelet in her hands. Ink stains her pale skin, but doesn't dim the sheen of the pearls. "What is one pearl worth?"

"We are the Daughters of the Moon. There are those who revere us and will refuse to take any payment. But there are also those who seek to gain profit from the distress of others, even ours. We may be able to count on goodwill, but we must prepare ourselves to also act cunningly when the need arises. One pearl is worth as much as those willing to help us decide."

The train shrieks a steamy hiss. Sibilia climbs on the divan, on her knees, and peeks out through the crack between the once-white curtains. As I am sitting opposite to her, I catch a glimpse as well.

This town of Fornavav is as I have read from the notes of the imperial messengers. Here houses beaten gray by the winds border the one narrow street. Farther away, small farms dot the flat fields that snow covers for half of the year. The sky is blue, cloudless. It is a cold and quiet day outside.

"We divide into our usual groups," I say. "Elise, you lead Merile and Alina."

"And Rafa and Mufu," Merile adds, squatting down to pet the dogs in turns. "Yes, my dear sillies, we would never abandon you!"

Sibilia rolls her eyes. She would be glad to leave the dogs here. Alone. Though fifteen and a half already, at times she acts immature. I can't count on her maturing fast enough to become an empress in the case . . . No, I will not think of that either. We should and we will adhere to the established routine. "Sibilia, you come with me."

As the train slows down, we lounge by the marble-topped table, waiting for the guards to come. Remnants of tea slosh in the cups. I catch a whiff of the smoky scent. It reminds me of the home we had to leave behind because I failed my family. The least I can do is to ensure that one day my sisters can return to the halls and hallways where they belong.

The train stutters to a halt. Tea spills over my cup's edge, onto the saucer. The stain is shaped like a crescent.

"What if they won't let us out?" Merile clutches Mufu against her chest. The charcoal gray dog licks her face with ardor. Sibilia cringes.

What if they don't? Then I will have to argue our way out. This is the plan I conceived the night the gagargi's spell broke. The letters I wrote in the carriage on my way back to the palace. The hawks I released to carry my plea to my seed. By coincidence and luck, both the ill kind and the good kind, the pieces that were missing earlier have somehow materialized.

Though my seed never replied. How could he? But in him I trust, for he is the one the Moon sent for my mother when I needed to be conceived.

"They will let us out," I say in such a serene tone that my sisters have no choice but to believe in me. This is the power I have. This is the power each one of them must eventually learn.

Minutes pass, and my heart races. What is taking the guards so long? Why haven't they come for us yet? Why has the established routine been broken?

My sisters trust in me. If I were to show any sign of nervousness or distress, they would soon lose their composure. I must not fidget with my bracelet. I must not smooth my hem too often. I may only continue to smile in the tranquil way that leads people to believe that I know more than they do, that indicates that everything is in order.

At last, the door creaks open. Captain Janlav enters, our blankets heaped over his arm. "Time for a brief walk, daughters."

Alina and Merile run to him. And he ... he laughs, head bent back, moustache vibrating. Elise, still sitting beside me, closes her eyes with a sigh so soft, so tender. Though Captain Janlav has forgotten her ... It is as if a part of my sister wants to stay with him. Even if he is our captor, and hence due to report everything he sees and hears to the gagargi.

"Here you go, little Daughter of the Moon." Captain Janlav hands Alina her blanket. Merile snatches hers from his arms. Rafa and Mufu bounce against him, waiting to be dressed up in their coats that are no longer quite white.

While Alina and Merile fuss with the dogs, I get up from my chair. Elise and Sibilia follow my example. I accept my blanket and so does Sibilia. But Elise halts before Captain Janlav and then slowly turns around as if she were waiting for him to wrap the blanket around her shoulders.

I don my blanket, curious to see if manners take precedence over his orders. I meet Elise's gaze, and it is a calculating one. She isn't doing this because she yearns for his attention. This is a test, I realize. To see if he ...

He helps my sister to position the blanket around her shoulders just so, eager to assist her when he can. It is sometimes easy to forget who he is. A turncoat. The man who betrayed my family. But his manners aren't ill. He believes in the cause that the gagargi whispered in the people's ear. He believes he is on the right side. I can't blame him for that.

"Are we ready now?" he asks. No doubt the other guards already await us on the platform. Belly and Beard smoke. Boots and Tabard jest. The guards are more relaxed now that we are far away from cities, the places where the revolution tore deep gashes. This far away no one cares. Whatever happens in the palaces, whoever leads the empire, nothing changes for people who live in the deep north.

We exit the train for what I hope is one last time. Just as I had expected, Belly and Beard smoke, Boots and Tabard huddle at the platform. There is no one waiting at the station, apart from a magpie, the bird black and white—and why would there be when the trains are scheduled to stop here only once a week? People here, they have learned that ignorance is bliss. As soon as they saw the train and the guards, they no doubt hurried inside, locked the doors, and shuttered the windows. They will not be peeping out before they hear the train depart.

The sun clings on the zenith, as high as it dares to climb during a winter day. It is freezing cold on the platform. The temperature sets against my ankles like icy chains. For surely it is that which weighs on my steps, and not guilt.

"Rafa and Mufu want to run around the station!" Merile announces. She is more cunning than I have given her credit for, it seems.

"Captain Janlav." Elise links her arm with him as if he were still courting her. She asks cheerily, "Shall we go and see how fast they can run?"

He chuckles, though frost already forms on his beard and moustache. "I don't see why not."

But he studies me for a moment too long, as if there were something he was about to say, that no one else will say. What can it be? Has he learnt of our plan? He doesn't say. He leaves with Elise, Merile, and Alina. The first part of the plan is set in motion.

I stroll down the length of the platform with Sibilia, the magpie hopping alongside us. Beard waddles behind us. I know it is him, though I can't see him. His breath always smells of raw onions.

"My stomach cramps," Sibilia says.

I hear Beard stumble, halt. He doesn't want to hear a single thing more about Sibilia's wretched days. She excels in describing them. She has had a lot of practice. This, too, is a routine we have carefully built up, a topic of conversation we know the guards don't want to overhear.

We reach the end of the platform and the narrow plank stairs there. I barely dare to glance to my left, at the stables that should be there, for the person who should be waiting for us. For it is such a long time since I wrote the letters, since my hawks flew off. So many weeks separate us from that night. Is it really possible that a plan conceived in such a way could work?

"There's someone waving at you," Sibilia whispers, plump cheeks glowing red.

It is only then that I dare to look.

The man dressed in a wolf's fur coat tends to the brown horses harnessed before a troika even as he waves at me. His collars are drawn up against his bearded cheeks, but his cap doesn't quite hide his missing eye and the scarred face. It is my seed, General Monzanov, but I can't afford to bask in joy even for one heartbeat.

"Why, is it really . . ." Sibilia's voice trails off. She can't quite believe what she is seeing either. She rubs her eyes, the movement already clumsy from the cold.

But as my sisters so often remind me, my mind is ever cold and rational. This isn't as I planned. There is but one troika waiting for us, and the three horses munch hay contently as if they had been about it for hours already with no end in sight to their blessing. Where are the soldiers ready to escort my sisters and me to safety? There, by the stable, two astride chestnut horses, two on the ground, cigarettes jutting out from the corners of their mouth. They wear lamb fur coats and red gloves. Are they loyal to my seed or someone else?

General Monzanov waves again. Why is he drawing attention to himself? The smell of raw onions reveals Beard approaching Sibilia and me. What should I do? Ignore my seed or acknowledge him?

"What is General Monzanov doing here?" I wonder aloud as if I were puzzled to see him.

Beard strokes his chin, and I am not sure if he is doubting my performance or equally confused by the general's presence. Eventually he says, "Your seed bears a message to you."

This is the time I must remain calm so that the cogs and wheels of my mind can spin fast rather than be jammed by emotions of any sort. If Beard knows that General Monzanov bears a message to me, this means that one of the guards—Captain Janlav, no doubt—noticed him as soon as the train halted and has talked with him. This must be why it took the guards longer than usual to let us out. Was talking to the guards my seed's idea, or has something gone terribly wrong? Why do I think it might be the latter? There is only one way to find out.

"Then I shall go and talk with him," I say to Beard. I brush

Sibilia's arm as I pass her. "Wait here."

I stride down the creaking plank stairs, sabots clacking.

As I wade through the snowy path, toward the stable, I catch a glimpse of Elise, Merile, and Alina. She still clings to Captain Janlav's arm as if she had a hard time staying up on the icy street. The dogs dash from Alina to Merile, bringing back twigs that the girls toss at them. Elise veers to a halt as she notices me alone. I swing my right hand up as if I had slipped and needed to balance myself, a sign agreed on beforehand. She should delay on the street. She doesn't yet know it, but we might need to soon part ways with each other.

For my seed has brought with him only one troika. It can't fit the six of us. If it comes to choosing between some of us fleeing or all of us staying... During the five long weeks of solitude, I have considered every eventuality. I have already reached the decision that is by no means easy but the best of our available options.

If need be, I will remain behind. Elise and the girls shall go with my seed. Elise understands my people. Merile and Alina are the youngest. And there is the sad truth that I can but acknowledge. As the witch warned me, the price for bleeding away the gagargi's seed is high. I may not be able to have other children, though only years may reveal the true state of matters.

I glance over my shoulder, though I know I shouldn't. Sibilia shivers on the platform, gray blanket folded tight against her chest, with only the magpie as her company. My poor sister, she is still but a girl, and yet there is nothing I can do for her. To save Elise and the little girls, I will have to sacrifice Sibilia's freedom. It isn't fair of me to decide for her, but this isn't something I could exactly have asked her opinion about either. If she knew, she would only hate me.

As I approach my seed, the wrongness intensifies. The reins of the brown horses are tied to a wooden rail. Why would someone preparing for a speedy departure do so? Closer still, I notice no belt cinches my seed's coat, and I can't see the telltale bulge of a sword either. No strap of a rifle runs across his chest. He is unarmed—why? To deceive the train guards into thinking that he is on the same side? Mother always said that hope isn't something an empress can count on. It isn't the wind that chills me, but recalling her sober tone.

"Celestia," my seed greets me when I am a mere ten steps away. He spreads his arms wide, palms up. The movement is stiff, as if he were wounded. His smile betrays nothing, but his gray eyes reveal his pain.

"General Monzanov . . ." I can't quite hold on to my composure. I dash to him, through the crunching, ice-crusted snow. For this is the man I have always been able to rely on. It is he who sided with the gagargi because that is what I asked of him. It is he who has now forsaken the same man, simply because I sent him a letter.

My seed clasps his arms around me. I bury my head against his shoulder, the snow-dusted wolf fur that smells of smoke and gunpowder. He has come to set us free. With his help, I will reclaim my empire. With . . .

"Celestia," he whispers. And there it is again, the wrongness.

I don't want to break the embrace. But my own needs or wishes bear secondary priority to those of my empire. Even if the train guards believe my seed to be on the same side, the sooner we are on our way, the higher the likelihood that at least a part of the plan will work.

I steel myself and say what needs to be said. "Untie the

horses. Take Elise and the girls. I will remain behind and delay the pursuit, no matter the cost."

He steps away from me then, and this single act of rejection hurts my heart, my body, as if I were a creature of glass fracturing against granite. "No."

His gaze is very gray, pale as icicles. I meet his eyes, dreading what I might see. What is the reason behind his refusal? Has the gagargi tampered with his soul as he once did with mine? I know now what to look for, the absence of emotion, of memory. But my seed's gaze is bright, his own. He isn't under the gagargi's power.

"Why?" I ask, unsure of how much time we have left. Elise still lingers at the street with the girls. Sibilia paces back and forth on the platform, the magpie skimming beside her. Belly and Tabard have joined Beard. My sister will soon grow afraid of them and dart to me. Of that I am sure.

"The Crescent Empress is dead. General Kravakiv has been defeated. Every noble close to you or your mother has been either converted or executed." My seed's voice is level, that of a man who has delivered bad news to his empress too many times to count. "Gagargi Prataslav learned of our plan. I don't know how. It doesn't matter now. My men and I were ambushed yesterday, just a mile away from this village. I was captured. My company was rounded up and shot before my eyes. One after another."

I can see the blood staining the snow, the smoke parting after gunfire, even without closing my eyes. And closing my eyes would benefit no one. I can only consider the facts and try and craft a new plan. "The soldiers by the stable?"

My seed glances at the red-gloved soldiers. He shrugs as if they didn't matter. Perhaps they don't. "They have their orders.

They are beyond reasoning with. It is as you said. Their minds are not their own."

My stomach clenches, a pain trivial compared to that which I had to suffer to rid myself of Gagargi Prataslav's seed. He has grown powerful indeed. How many men and women does he have fully in his control, with parts of their souls captured into glass beads?

"What are their orders?" I ask, refusing to give up. For fear can only cloud one's mind, and that is something I will never again let happen to myself.

My seed pats the neck of the closest horse, a thick-furred brown mare tacked on the troika's left lead. He has always loved horses; the ones he owned, the ones that gave their lives in the battles, the ones he met just in passing. The mare swishes its tail and continues munching hay. My seed smiles faintly, but then his expression turns somber. "Once the train leaves, they will shoot me dead."

My heart sinks, for it is as if the ground were drawing me toward it, as if it were just a matter of seconds before it will swallow me altogether. My seed has calculated the odds and come to a grim conclusion. He has accepted his fate.

I will not resign myself to mine. Not before I have explored every possibility, no matter how unlikely they are to succeed.

"We do have one troika." I must hear his reasoning. I can't just welcome defeat, return with my sisters to the train, and leave him here to die.

"The gelding in the middle is lame. The troika's right runner is broken."

I shake my head despite myself. No wonder the soldiers by the stable are snickering. They know any attempt my seed were to make would be doomed to fail. They want to see him try,

I realize. And worse, the gagargi wants me to attempt to defy him.

If I were to try today, he would win. If I don't try, he will win. My prospects are bleak indeed.

"The gagargi wants me to tell you that you belong to him." My seed spits on the ground, the snow trampled ugly brown by hooves. He is disgusted by the words that he must part with. "The next time you try to flee, he will have one of your sisters shot."

My enemy knows me too well. I can see my life unfolding before me. He will blackmail me into appearing by his side and bearing his seed. Once he thought he could have me marry the Moon while spellbound to him. Now I doubt he will let any gagargi perform the ceremony, lest my father learn of his foul ways. I can live with my own pain, but not with the knowledge that further actions on my part will hurt my innocent sisters.

Elise has halted at the end of the street. She is waiting for my signal. But she has stared at me for too long, and this has intrigued Captain Janlav. He studies me, suspicious. Even Merile and Alina have noticed that the plan isn't progressing as it should. They no longer play with the dogs.

I wave at my sisters to return to the train. This plan is foiled beyond recovery. We must salvage what we can.

"I am proud of you, Celestia," General Monzanov says. Mother thought him the best strategist to have walked under the Moon for centuries. He knows when a defeat is inevitable. He doesn't waste time dwelling on it. "You have found yourself a formidable foe. Though the situation might seem bleak now, that it is not. You are a daughter of my seed. You are the empress-to-be. You will defeat the gagargi one day, and your victory shall be great."

My breathing comes in short gasps. I swallow back tears, the lump in my throat. He believes in me, the one who failed the empire. How can he be so sure of my victory, when even I doubt myself?

He places his palms on my shoulders and presses a kiss on my forehead. His gray beard tickles my skin. His frostbitten lips feel warm. This is how I must remember him. All this will be gone in mere moments.

"Go now, with your head held high. Take your place as the Moon's wife. You will come up with another plan. You will triumph. You will succeed."

I kiss his cheeks, twice on each side. Then I turn around and march back, following my own footprints. The icy wind chafes my face, my forehead, as if trying to erase his kiss. Tears burn in my eyes, but I will not cry them. Not now, not ever, for my sisters must not see me despair. I can't allow the guards see me waver either. There is a chance they don't know of what came and will come to pass, no matter how small that chance might be.

My sisters await me on the train platform with the guards in a crescent behind them. Elise's smile falters as she takes in my grim expression. Sibilia closes her eyes and sighs. Merile takes hold of Alina's hand. The dogs are curled at their feet.

"What news did your seed bring us?" Captain Janlav asks. "He said it was only for your ears, as ordered by Gagargi Prataslav himself."

How devious is this man that has become my enemy! How cruel he is, too, to let a man travel across half the empire to help the daughter of his seed, only to ambush him a day before, only to toy with him until the very end!

But I must be smarter than the gagargi is. For some reason,

he doesn't want the train guards to learn of the rescue attempt. It will benefit my sisters and me to keep it a secret as well—for if the guards were to learn that we tried to flee, they would search our cabins, even our personages, and no doubt confiscate the pearls and sequins, perhaps even the book of scriptures that Sibilia has filled with her thoughts.

But what news could have warranted sending my seed to us? From the corner of my eye, I glimpse the magpie again. It brings to my mind the story Elise relayed to me, and I know it then, the answer that will buy me more time to think. "The Crescent Empress is dead."

A gust of wind sweeps down the platform. It scatters specks of ice over us as it howls like an enraged beast. The guards' faces pale as one.

"Bless the Moon." Captain Janlav draws a circle around his heart. The other guards are quick to follow suit. They still respect and fear my father.

My sisters and I stand unfazed. We have known of our mother's demise for weeks now, ever since the shadow of a swan visited Alina. We have hidden our grief so well that unburying it is a struggle. At least one of us should cry and wail. But none of us do.

It is Alina who breaks the silence. "Are we going?"

I wrap an arm around her narrow shoulders. She doesn't realize how dangerous this question is. I can't chastise her for that. But I can minimize the damage. "Yes, my dear. We are going back to the train now."

As I lead Alina toward the day carriage, she glances over her shoulder. I shouldn't look back, but I do. My seed is petting the brown mare. The horse's head rests against his temple. His lips move as he murmurs soft words.

"Oh . . ." Alina stumbles on her own feet. "I thought . . ."

"Hush, little one. Hush now." I guide her toward the train. The guards must not learn why my seed really came. Secrets are valuable. Some more so than others. This one is particularly precious, a weapon against the gagargi. "We grieve for Mother when we are alone. That is the way of the Moon."

The wind moans as we return to our carriage. We don't. Captain Janlav collects our blankets. He leaves without a word said, without one last smile aimed at Elise. He locks the door behind him. I count the steps moving farther away. My sisters stare expectantly at me. I raise my right hand. I lower it only after I can no longer hear his steps.

I dread what else I might hear. Gunshots in the distance. The demise of my seed.

Mother also said that an empress should never live in fear. She must face the truth and bear the consequences. Even if she is the one who betrayed those she loves the most. "The gagargi learnt of my plan."

My sisters glance at each other. Not one of them knew of my seed's involvement. Not one of them can be blamed. I did my best, but that wasn't enough. But what sort of excuse is that! I failed them, and that is unforgivable.

Elise reaches out for my left hand. Her long, slim fingers curl around mine. "It's not your fault."

And then, without a word said, my sisters form a circle, from the oldest to the youngest, so that in the end I hold hands with both Elise and Alina. They . . . they haven't forgiven me, for they see no reason to do so in the first place. At that moment I am speechless.

The train shudders into movement. The clanks against the icy rails are loud and cold, slow and heavy. How long will the soldiers by the stable wait before executing my seed? Until the train recedes from sight or not even that long?

I wait for the sound of rifles fired, holding my breath until I grow dizzy. But the train is too loud today. It hoots, and the wheels clatter like the hooves of an iron steed. I will not hear when my seed's end comes. Perhaps it is better that way.

"What now?" Sibilia's cheeks are flushed red, but her voice is soft and mellow. Merile and Alina nod in unison. The dogs lie down against my feet, to rest. They are not worried about what the future might bring in its wake. My sisters, they trust me with their lives, and as I am the oldest, it is my duty to come up with a new plan, to prevail against odds that might yet seem impossible.

"We will wait. We will be patient." I squeeze Alina's hand, Elise's hand. Theirs are so warm against mine. "We are the Daughters of the Moon. Eventually we will triumph."

About the Author

Photograph by Writers of the Future

LEENA LIKITALO hails from Finland, the land of endless summer days and long, dark winter nights. She lives with her husband on an island at the outskirts of Helsinki, the capital. But regardless of her remote location, stories find their way to her and demand to be told.

While growing up, Leena struggled to learn foreign languages. At sixteen, she started reading science fiction and fantasy in English. The stories were simply too exciting not to finish, and thus she rather accidentally learned the language.

These days, Leena breaks computer games for a living. When she's not working, she writes obsessively. And when she's not writing, she can be found at the stables riding horses.

TOR·COM

Science fiction. Fantasy. The universe. And related subjects.

*

More than just a publisher's website, *Tor.com* is a venue for **original fiction, comics,** and **discussion** of the entire field of SF and fantasy, in all media and from all sources. Visit our site today—and join the conversation yourself.